*Sweet Summer
and Other Stories*

"Sweet Summer" was originally written for *Fastfood Fiction: Short Stories To Go*, edited by Noelle de Jesus-Chua, and published by Anvil Publishing, Inc in 2003. However, it first appeared in *Heights* (v XLVIII, 3, 2001), and was later anthologized in *The Likhaan Book of Poetry and Fiction 2001*, edited by Gémino H Abad and Cristina Pantoja Hidalgo, and published by the UP Press in 2002.

"Saints and Souls" first appeared in *Heights* (v XLVI, 1, 1998), and was later anthologized in *The Likhaan Book of Poetry and Fiction 1998*, edited by J Neil C Garcia and Charlson Ong, and published by the UP Press in 2000.

"The Skylab" first appeared in *Creative Juices: Works of the Ateneo Faculty*, edited by Susan Evangelista and published by DIWA Scholastic Press in 2001.

"Trouble and Tears" first appeared in the August issue of *The Diliman Review*, (v 51, 4, 2004).

Sweet Summer and Other Stories

Cyan Abad-Jugo

The University of the Philippines Press
Diliman, Quezon City
2004

THE UNIVERSITY OF THE PHILIPPINES PRESS
E. de los Santos St., UP Campus, Diliman, Quezon City 1101
Tel. No.: 9253243 / Telefax No.: 9282558
E-mail: press@up.edu.ph; uppress@uppress.org
Website: www.uppress.org

© 2004 by Cyan Abad-Jugo
All rights reserved. No part of this publication may be reproduced, stored in a retrieval system, or transmitted, in any form or by any means, electronic, mechanical, photocopying, and/or otherwise, without the prior permission of the author.

Philippine Writers Series 2004
In cooperation with LIKHAAN:
The UP Institute of Creative Writing

Book Design by Arwin U. Ayson
Illustrations by Ranol

ISBN 971-542-446-5

Printed in the Philippines by the UP Press Printery Division

for my #1 hero and wizard,
Jimmy Abad,
and my #1 love and jester,
Micho Jugo

Contents

Thanks / ix

Sweet Summer / 2
Nose Aches / 6
Saints and Souls / 22
Trouble and Tears / 38
The Skylab / 50
Kapayapaan Lobby / 72
The Grand Jeté / 86
A Cinderella Soap / 92
The Line / 108
The Patient / 124
The Abominable Snowman / 158

The Author / 179
The Artist / 179

Thanks

For the space, solitude, and sustenance they provided, I would like to thank the director, the admissions committee, and the staff (Amy, Margaret, Jane, and Kerry) at the Hawthornden Castle International Retreat for Writers, Scotland.

Thank you too, Chris Humphreys, Tim Liardet, and Igor Sachnovsky, for even more sustenance and encouragement.

Thank you, dad, my walking dictionary, encyclopedia, history book, grammar check, and writing guru. I'd be lost without you!

For their spirit of abundance and generosity, thank you to the mothers and teachers around me: my supermother, Mercy Abad, my second mothers, Edna Manlapaz and Josie Banaag, my new mother, Ginny Jugo; my grade school teachers Mrs Otero, Mrs Francisco, and Mrs Cutiongco; my make-believe mothers, Mummy Kyrie, Auntie Ysa, and Mama Rica; my college and grad school mentors and teachers: Prof Eric Torres,

Ma'am Beni, Jovi Miroy, Tita Marj, Tito NVM, Fr Joseph Galdon, SJ, Fr Asandas Balchand, SJ, Dr Susan Evangelista, and Dr Ediboy Calasanz; Susan Bloom, Cathie Mercier, and Nancy Bond; Tita Jing, Tito Butch, Tito Krip, Tito Franz, Tita Ching, Prof Isabel Huggan, Dr Judy Ick, and Prof Thelma Arambulo.

For giving me tons of memories to write about, and for dealing with my disappearing acts, thank you to my growing up buddies the Bugoys, the Happy Club, and the Living Colors/Bugoys2; thank you to my friends, Haydee, Eppie, Prudy, Ate Meng, Jean, Miguel, Rica, Paul, Arlene, Marianne, Gladys, Cholo, Chona, BJ, Ron, Larry, Vince, Munik, Noni, Daisy, Annagee, Lissa, Badong, Louise, Robby, Cecile, Cindy-Unicorn, MishMash, Kix and Fosco; thank you to my grad school pals, Elizabeth, Caty, Deborah, Lori, Akiko, Ya-Hui, Kathleen, Cynthia, Tylka, Trina, Lorraine, Kirsten, Liz, and the Stanfields; thank you to Micho's friends, the Abnoys and the Bwaks.

Most especially, thank you to my family the Abads and Riveras and Jugos, my extended family the Castillos and Gils and Estreras, for bearing with my absentmindedness and my periods of invisibility and staring into space. Special thanks go to Papa Bert for laughing away the iced tea I spilled on him the first time I sat down to dinner with the Jugos; and special thanks to Cybele, Diego, and David who

Thanks

have had to live all their lives with an ate who has a short attention span.

And thank you Micho-potpot, clown and confidant, for the glorious mess, the sound effects, the cymbals clanging in my ears, and the singing in the bathroom.

Oops, I'm sure I forgot to mention others. Thanks guys.

Sweet Summer and Other Stories

Sweet Summer

The Candy Club were all twelve that summer, sitting every afternoon on the village's water tank, savoring macaroons, Halls honey-lemon, and Cloud 9. The older boys had begun to hover about like bees, ogling them like treats—but only the two creamy long-legged eclairs, not the nut-brown fudge in a housedress melting in the sun.

One day, before the boys zoomed in, a younger boy approached with his Doberman, reaching for the faucet.

"Think of worms, of diarrhea," Camilla said, nose addressing the still air.

The boy looked up and considered the three girls, none of them looking. The dog ignored them, and lapped at the water flowing into the boy's hand. The boy splashed some on his face and hair, then straightened up, letting the water drip.

"Aachoo!" Faye winked at the bright sky.

Sara could not bear it, and turned her raisin eyes upon the boy.

His hand shot out at once, dirt under fingernails, but she bent and took it.

"Frederick," he said, "and Dolby." He indicated the dog.

Camilla and Faye tittered, now regarding him. "That's Sara the Square you're shaking hands with."

Sara hunched up. "You live here?" she asked, and he nodded. "I'll walk with you."

Camilla and Faye snorted. The boy shrugged. The dog loped off.

"Frederick, walk your two dogs!" Camilla ventured. Laughter. High fives.

Sara slid off the tank, cement scraping the back of her thighs. She ran to take her place beside the boy and his dog.

The nut-brown fudge regarded herself with surprise. A boy, even though he was only around eleven, was talking, walking, with her! She offered Frederick a choice of sweets. He picked the honey-lemon. Good, since she wanted the Cloud 9.

Sara bounced, smearing her fingers with chocolate. Her glee rubbed off on Dolby, who ran and pounced. She lay pinned to the sharp grass, blades pricking through her housedress. Dolby started licking. She laughed and tried to shoo him, accidentally touching his nose. He chased her fingers. Frederick whistled, and the weight that was Dolby left her. Frederick offered his hand the second time that day, and for a while, she forgot the brown face, pudgy hands, and squarish body.

"Don't walk alone at night," Frederick warned. "People can jump at you like Dolby did." Frederick sprang and rolled on the grass, demonstrating. Dolby barked twice and followed. Sara watched both of them—one, then the other—and wished it had been the boy who had jumped at her and not the dog.

She offered him her hand. After all, he had given his. When he stood up, his lemony breath touched her face, and her heart leapt as if she had been kissed. He didn't let go her hand either. He bowed and danced her about in a jerky sort of dance, Dolby snapping at their heels. Then it ended, grins spreading on both their faces.

"What was that shit?"

They let go at once. Felix. Sara recognized him.

"Nothing, Kuya," Frederick replied, choking. He cleared his throat and spat a sliver of honey-lemon. It glistened gold on the pavement before Dolby licked it off.

Felix laughed and cuffed his brother. "You're a natural! I'm proud of you! Now let me introduce you to some real yummies over there…"

Off they went the way Frederick and Sara had come, but forgetting Sara. Only the dog looked back, licking his nose.

Nose Aches

Kuya Jinny's cologne has taken away all the air in the bathroom. It smells sweet and heavy so it's hard for me to breathe while brushing my teeth.

Mommy laughs when she sees me stumbling out the door holding my nose. "Your kuya has fallen in love," she says, "and now he has to smell good."

I think I like the smell of the sun better—the smell of grass, wind, and heat. Kuya Jinny smells like the sun after his soccer practice in school, or after he goes out with his gang in our village.

As we stand outside our gate, waiting for the schoolbus, and before our neighbor Erwin appears, I ask him, "Are you in love, Kuya Jin? Mommy says you are."

Kuya Jinny squints his black eyes, and his little nose grows twice its size when he snorts. "Mom doesn't know anything." He ruffles his hair impatiently.

A whiff of cologne hits me full in the face, prompting me to continue. "How come you bought the Eternity then?"

He sets his chin. "I wanted to," he replies. "Leave me alone."

Kuya Jinny says things he really doesn't mean, but Erwin comes, so I do have to leave him alone. He doesn't want to be bothered when his friends are around. Other times, he lets me borrow his tapes to play on his stereo, and we dance in his room, or we watch TV cartoons together. He shares his *X-Men* comics with me too, as long as I wash my hands first and I take care not to crumple them.

Kuya Jinny is expensive, Daddy says. He likes to collect lots of rock and rap music, and to wear Cole Haan shoes, Polo shirts, and Calvin Klein jeans, when he doesn't have to wear the school uniform. He insists on wearing white shirts under his polo, no matter how hot it is, and Mommy complains about how much laundry soap he uses up.

Last week he bought the bottle of Eternity cologne. Usually, he saves his allowance to buy Marvel and DC comics, and GameBoy cartridges. He saves and then spends even more money than Ate Wen, who always wants more and more clothes, because she goes to college, and they don't wear uniforms in college. I don't have any savings at all. Mommy says I will get a real allowance in grade five. Now I only have enough to buy a juice drink, and I have to eat whatever Nana Luz packs in my lunchbox for me.

Nose Aches

"Yo Jin," Erwin whacks Kuya Jinny on the back. I start sneezing. The Eternity has found its way up my nose.

Erwin watches me as Kuya Jinny whacks him back. "What's the matter with Siopao here?" He always calls me that because I have a round face, like the white bread of the siopao. I don't care. He's not handsome like Kuya Jinny, anyway. Kuya Jinny has thick black eyebrows, dark sparkling eyes, and smooth fair skin. Erwin has red spots all over his face, crooked teeth, and messy hair that doesn't spike because it curls at the ends.

When the schoolbus arrives, they take their place at the very back. I go to my usual seat in the bus' belly, between the window and Vince, who has saved me my spot. Behind us, Erwin and Kuya Jinny suddenly make grunting noises, while they wrestle each other. Erwin still hasn't noticed how Kuya Jinny smells, but I sense that the bus is filling up with the scent of Eternity.

"Please stop that, you two," Mang Doming, the driver, calls from the front of the bus. "You hurt anyone back there and I knock both of you down!"

Erwin and Kuya Jinny sit up, arms still around each other, grinning at the rest of us. The older girls seated in front of the bus don't look back at them. And we see Erwin whisper something to Kuya Jinny that makes him turn red and poke Erwin in the side with his bad finger. Now they are poking each other with bad fingers. I know using the tall finger is a bad sign, but I never tell Mommy the bad signs and words that Kuya Jinny uses when she isn't around. Kuya Jinny knows that I can keep secrets. So I don't think Kuya Jinny is in love. He would have told me.

"I don't like wrestling, it is such a rough sport," Nathan comments from across the aisle.

"It's fake," Vince says beside me. I turn back to look at the X-Men figures Vince has brought today in his bag—Cyclops, who wears funny-looking red glasses, and Rogue, who can absorb and weaken the powers of anyone.

"Hey Vince," I say, "Cyclops and Rogue aren't partners."

"I know," he answers, turning his back on Nathan, "but I thought you liked Rogue best. So we can play during recess."

"It's all an act, pulling a flea-flicker on us," continues Nathan. He never seems to know when we're listening and when we're not. He likes to use big words too, words nobody understands. And he already turned ten last June, a week after classes began.

Vince is smart too, but he's very quiet in class. The teachers all say that Vince and I are the quietest. Maybe that is also why we are best friends.

When the bus stops, I hurry out. I want to shake off Kuya Jinny's new smell. I watch him and Erwin stride away to the seventh grade wing, arms still around each other, laughing loudly.

Nose Aches

∽ ∾

I have known Vince since grade one. We somehow always got into the same section together. When we began grade four this year, we were allowed to choose our own seats. Vince and I agreed to sit in the second row, but he wanted to sit near the middle, and I wanted to sit near the window. There was an empty desk between us, and while we were still trying to decide who would take it and give up the middle or the window seat, somebody crashed into it and grinned up at us.

The person was Tracy, someone who usually stayed by herself and moved away from giggly girls. We were both very surprised, and I could see that Vince was a bit frightened, because Tracy was bigger and older than us. But Tracy laughed out loud, and Vince started to laugh too.

"You are a great problem-solver," Vince said.

And Tracy replied, "I know."

She really did know how to solve many problems, like how to get away from Nathan, and how to get better lunches by sharing what we brought from home and bought from the cafeteria. And then, this week, she thought about playing X-Men.

Kuya Jinny has only one figurine, Colossus, who looks like a giant, muscular mummy. I knew from the start that he would not lend it to me, although he says he's too old for toys. He never takes it down from his comic book shelf either. When I asked for my own X-Men action figure, Daddy told me they were only for boys, even when I said Rogue was a girl. So now Vince has to lend me his Rogue.

When the bell rings for recess, Tracy scoots us to the further part of the cafeteria, where the grade six and seven students hang out, away from all the food stalls and lines. "Let's take advantage of our small height." She winks at Vince. "And be virtually invisible."

"You sound like Nathan," Vince says, to annoy her back. Vince is sensitive about his height, even if he is an inch taller than me. We have the same shoe size, and he is smaller than Tracy, who almost reaches Kuya Jinny's chin.

I follow Tracy to a table and sit beside her. Vince hands me the Rogue figurine. We look around first, checking if any of the older grades have noticed our invasion. But they are busy talking to each other. Tracy shakes her head sadly and claps her pudgy hands over her ears. The older girls giggle worse than the girls in grade four.

"Let's start with the part when Jean Grey turns into the Dark Phoenix," Vince suggests, because the Dark Phoenix is Tracy's action figure. He has to repeat it for Tracy, when she uncovers her ears.

"Don't mind them Trace," I whisper, and I also have to repeat myself because the table behind me bursts into loud

Nose Aches

laughter. Vince and Tracy look over my shoulder curiously. Before I even turn around fully, I smell him.

Kuya Jinny is slapping hands with his friends. Erwin puts an arm around him and whispers something.

"All right, all right," Kuya Jinny says, straightening his polo. All the other boys around him clap, and someone with glasses says, "Go Jinny."

Kuya Jinny never even sees me as he circles our table and two others until he reaches the pizza stall, where three girls stand. He talks to one who has long hair tied with a pink ribbon, and she shakes her head. The ponytail sways gracefully. Kuya Jinny talks again. He is smiling and reaching for his back pocket. Kuya Jinny rarely smiles, he either just laughs loudly, or snorts and frowns. The girl lifts her two hands like she is giving up.

Behind me, everyone is quiet. I know they are watching too. Someone claps softly. Then I hear Erwin say, "I told you he'd do it. I told you he'd take the dare." I can tell it's Erwin because of the squeaky, high-and-low voice.

Then another person says, "Only because he likes her, pare. Jinny wouldn't treat out just anyone."

Vince, Tracy, and I are still watching Kuya Jinny. He slides his wallet smoothly into his pants' back pocket, and the girl takes a slice of pizza from the vendor. Then they walk away with the two other girls following, whispering and giggling behind them.

"Putcha, he's not coming back here!"

The bad word makes Vince and Tracy turn to look at whoever said it, but I'm not so interested.

"What on earth was that?" Tracy asks.

I shrug, and then we start to play the X-Men.

෴

When I see Kuya Jinny, I leave Vince and Tracy in the lunch line and run.

"Kuya Jin, Kuya Jinny!"

Many people turn to look at me, and I stop in my tracks. But Kuya Jinny has heard me, and whirls about with the rest of his friends.

"What?" he demands, crossing his arms. His chin hardens into a straight line.

All his friends watch me, and some are smiling.

"Hey, Siopao!" Erwin greets me, and then the others laugh and say "Hello Siopao" too. The guy in the glasses is the only one who says "Hi Bing!"

A group of grade four boys pass between me and Kuya Jinny, but Kuya Jinny doesn't try to leave. He's frowning something awful now, and threading his way to me, while waving his friends away. "I'll follow," he calls to them. Then he faces me. "What do you want?"

His arms remain crossed.

"I want a Coke," I say.

"Coke."

Daddy doesn't approve of Coke. He says we won't grow up if we keep drinking it. But I know what to tell Kuya Jinny. "How come you buy it all the time?"

He stiffens and catches sight of his friends, who are waving and pointing. Both Kuya Jinny and I follow their fingers, but I don't see what they are all looking at until I notice a girl behind a table sit up and smile. It's the girl with the pink ribbon. Her friends smile and wave too.

Kuya Jinny's chin softens as his lips wobble into a smile.

"Kuya Jin," I cry, tugging at his arm.

He snatches his arm away and glances in the direction of the girls. Then he places his hands on my cheeks and bends real close to my face, stifling me all of a sudden. "All right Bing-Bang, you asked for it. But don't blame me if you stay a midget the rest of your life."

He walks me to the stall with the softdrink vendo machine. I try to put my arm around him, but he pushes me too roughly by the shoulder and I stumble.

"Watch it," he snaps.

"Don't hurry me."

"Well you're such a slowpoke."

"You just want to be with the girl. Are you in love with her?"

He tightens his grip on my shoulder until I yell, "Ow!" and then he lets go. When the vendor puts the Coke on the countertop, Kuya Jinny ignores it, looking at the girls again. I stand on tiptoe and the Coke spills.

"Shit!" Kuya Jinny jumps back. "I hate you, Bing," he mutters. And then someone calls out his name.

It's the girl with the pink ribbon again. She walks towards us, smiling, and Kuya Jinny smiles back, his hand pushing at my shoulder. When she turns to me, I stick my tongue out and run away.

When classes are done for the day, we have to wait two hours for the schoolbus. Most of the grade seven students still have one more class, or like Kuya Jinny, they have varsity practice.

Tracy and Vince look pleased with my idea that our X-Men team has a mission among the rafters of the soccer field. But when we get there, we find the girl with the pink ribbon, and a lot of Kuya Jinny's classmates, sitting nearby. They cheer for Kuya Jinny's team. From time to time she stands up, waving something rolled up in her hand. During a short break, Kuya Jinny joins them. He does not even realize I'm there.

Beside me, Tracy becomes impatient. "What is wrong with you, Bing? You've been quiet for so long and Rogue doesn't

Nose Aches

talk at all like that." Her eyes flash and her mouth curls as she presses her lips closed. I know she is trying to keep her temper.

Vince moves closer to me. He knits his brows and shakes his head at Tracy. "We'll pretend that Rogue is not feeling well in this episode," he says.

"Maybe she did something bad," Tracy suggests.

Vince shakes his head again. I look at some of the girls near us, whispering. Kuya Jinny and his friends lean closer, trying to listen in on them. The girls laugh, trying to shoo them away. A girl makes a face after she touches Kuya Jinny's shirt, shrieking that it is wet with icky stuff. Kuya Jinny doesn't get angry at all. He laughs along with the rest of them and moves closer to frighten the girl.

"Maybe she messed up with Storm's tornadoes," Tracy continues.

"No, she's just sick—"

"Well," I say, and both Vince and Tracy turn to me. "Colossus gets mad at Rogue. She accidentally drained all his powers and made him look stupid in front of enemies."

Vince nods, but Tracy looks skeptical. "In front of enemies? Then he'd have been captured."

"Okay, so in front of the younger X-Men students then, and Prof Xavier," Vince puts in.

I want to change everything and start our episode again, but Tracy begins to hammer her Phoenix on the metal step above her. It's her sign that Jean Grey has transformed into the Dark Phoenix. I swallow and make Rogue run. "Okay, I'm on my way to say sorry to Colossus."

"You better," Vince says, eyeing the Dark Phoenix warily. "Then you can meet me ... I mean, Cyclops ... in the Danger Room and we can practice our fighting moves. Suppose Nightcrawler and Wolverine are there already?"

The sudden screams of the grade seven girls send Tracy's hands to her ears again. We watch as one girl starts to run after some boys. "Barbarians." Tracy rolls her eyes and groans, and then gives Dark Phoenix one last thump on the head.

෴

I look out the window, just like Erwin at the back of the bus, for a sign of Kuya Jinny. Erwin plays soccer too, but just for fun. He doesn't play for the varsity team like Kuya Jinny. For once he is quiet, but Nathan isn't.

"No," he says, "we don't get tornadoes in the Philippines. We get typhoons, monsoon rains, but not tornadoes. Have you ever seen *The Wizard of Oz*?"

"No," Vince says, "but Tracy and I were talking about Storm's powers. Don't you know the X-Men?"

"So you were talking in Social Studies, and about comics too. Don't you know they warp the mind?"

Nose Aches

"Yo, Jinny!" Erwin roars, and the few of us inside the bus all jump a little. Mang Doming standing just outside scowls towards Erwin's window.

Kuya Jinny, in his black and green soccer uniform, lifts his hand, but he is looking at someone behind him. It's the girl with the pink ribbon, again, and she only reaches up to his shoulder. That might make her only an inch taller than me.

She's still holding something rolled up in her hand, and this time, I recognize it: Kuya Jinny's *Batman* comics. He doesn't see what she's doing, so he doesn't yell at her the way he yelled at me once. What a barbarian. And then he forgets to get it as he waves at her and boards the bus. She stuffs it into her bag. Thief!

Vince and Nathan stop arguing when I stand and scramble past Vince. Vince protests when I step on his foot, but I don't care. I meet Kuya Jinny in the aisle and before I can think of words to say, I hug him and his sports bag, feeling sorry for the way he will cry later on over his crumpled comics. Poor Kuya Jinny. And then I don't want to let go, realizing he might still be angry with me.

"What's the matter with old Siopao there?" I hear Erwin ask.

But Kuya Jinny has hugged me back, one short quick hug, then drags me with him towards the back of the bus. He doesn't hate me. He sometimes just says things he doesn't mean.

"Lynette," he calls out.

The girl with the pink ribbon stands outside. She has not moved from where Kuya Jinny left her.

"My sister," Kuya Jinny points, at the same time pushing me forward. My face squashes a little onto the screen.

"Hello," she waves. "How cute!" She reminds me of Ate Wen, except that she is even smaller.

The bus starts to move. Everyone has boarded, and is chatting among friends. Only Vince looks at us, at me. Then he smiles, and I smile, and he turns away. Mang Doming calls from up front, "Sit down at the back!"

"Bye," Lynette calls. "Will return it to you tomorrow."

"Take your time," Kuya Jinny yells back, right in my ear. Then he sits down, and I fall on the seat beside him as the bus roars down the road. I search Kuya Jinny's face quickly, trying to see if he is angry with me, but he is smiling to himself. Erwin also looks at him, then crosses his eyes at me.

"Wow, pare," Kuya Jinny sighs, "she's pretty." He is talking to Erwin, I know, but he puts an arm around me.

Erwin groans and crosses his eyes some more. "You got it bad, man."

Nose Aches

Kuya Jinny shrugs. Suddenly he grabs me in a bear hug and whoops. "Yeah!" My face drags across his shirt and the number 11. My breath runs out.

When he lets go, I know my hair is messed up and my nose is red. It feels a little sore, but at the tip of it is Kuya Jinny's smell, a bit of the sun, and a bit like Eternity.

Saints and Souls

When November begins, we go to the cemetery instead of school. Most of the families go there on November 1, on All Saints' Day, but we go the day after, on All Souls' Day. I guess that means there are more saints than souls, and Kuya Miguel is only a soul. He died before Kuya Jinny was born, when Ate Wen was only two. He got sick because he was too young out of Mommy's stomach, and he never got well again.

"He's dead, so he shouldn't mind if I don't go," Ate Wen tells me, when I peep into the room we share, to tell her everyone else is already waiting for her. "And he's better off dead too, considering what kind of family he has." She's sitting on her bed with her arms crossed, and still without shoes.

"Watch what you're saying, dudette, he could have been my buddy," Kuya Jinny says from behind me.

"YOU better watch your street language with me, asshole,"

Ate Wen says right back, but she puts on her pumps. Then she starts brushing her straight, long hair. I wish I had hair like Ate Wen, black and shiny all the time. She described mine once as a mop that someone had dropped on my ears, right after she cut it so I wouldn't have trouble combing out the tangles in the morning.

Kuya Jinny leans on the doorframe after he pushes me into the room. He fingers the tuck of his red Giordano and traces the buckle of his belt. "What are you so grumpy about anyway?" he asks Ate Wen. "I'm sure the dead will not mind if you're not up to your usual standard of beautiful. Or is your new guy coming over again, what's his face … Manny?"

"He's not my new guy, he's just a friend," Ate Wen snaps. "But we had plans for today, and as usual, Mom botches it up."

"Well you should know we always go on the second. Was there ever a time we didn't?"

"I'm old enough to say if I want to go to the cemetery or not!" Ate Wen slams her brush down hard on the dresser and glares at Kuya Jinny.

"ROWENA," Mommy calls from downstairs. "KIDS—JIN-JIN, BING—WHERE ARE YOU? Hurry up, your father's waiting."

Kuya Jinny puts his arms around me and leads me out,

saying over his shoulder, "You better hurry, Wendy-dear, Dad'll be mad and bad." He never calls her *Ate*. He comes up with all these other funny names instead.

He hurries me down the stairs, and I scream and start laughing, out of breath by the time we come face to face with Mommy. She rests one fat elbow on the banister as she watches us. Her eyes have dark bruise-like circles under them.

"There you are, I thought you two were already waiting with Daddy."

"Dad told me to go look for the princess, she's taking so long."

Mommy sets a foot down on the first step. "I'll talk to her."

"Ate Wen is angry, Mommy, and she said a bad word," I say, following Kuya Jinny to the garage where Daddy sits in his white Mercedes that he always asks Kuya Jinny to wipe.

"What a tattletale you are, Bing-bang," Kuya Jinny scolds.

I want to shout something back, but Daddy's face silences me. His eyes look like stones from behind his thick black eyebrows. His huge hands clench and unclench the steering wheel. Daddy presses down on the horn.

We sit as Mommy hurries to the other side of the car and takes the front seat. The death seat, Daddy calls it, because if a car hits ours, the person sitting there would be in the most danger. He told us this when Kuya Jinny and Ate Wen kept quarreling about who would sit in front, closest to the radio. Now the death seat is Mommy's seat and nobody breaks that rule. I think Mommy is brave just to sit there and not be scared. She's not scared of Daddy either.

After a little more time, Ate Wen comes out of the kitchen door and sits behind Mommy, slamming the door hard. Daddy glares at her from the rear-view mirror and then starts the car. Nobody says anything until we leave the village, and, after some turns, enter the South Super Highway. Loyola Memorial is all the way in Marikina, very far from Alabang, where we live.

"This is tradition," Daddy begins quietly, "not only for our family but for most Filipinos. It's important that we keep it." He looks like Kuya Jinny, with dark brown hair, although Daddy's is longer, combed down smoothly to the right and peppered with white strands.

Ate Wen glares at his back. Her eyes look like Daddy's. "Tradition? We should have gone yesterday then," Ate Wen whispers resentfully, but Daddy hears her.

"The second is just as good as the first of November. If you only read the papers or listened to the news, you'd have an idea what the traffic was like yesterday."

"Nobody moved for hours on end," Mommy adds. "We'd all have melted with the heat and the jeepney fumes." She turns to look at us, then smiles like she wants to joke. "Think of poor Miguel," she begins. "He's just waiting and waiting for us to visit him."

Nobody smiles back at her. We have all heard the choking in her voice. She faces front again, but not before we see her blink a few times.

"God, this is sick," Ate Wen mutters. "Masochistic. One person dies and we have to be guilty for making him wait. Well, we're coming, Miguel, we're coming."

"What was that?" Daddy asks, raising his voice.

Nobody answers.

∽ ∾

When I open my eyes, I realize that Daddy has already stopped the car and stepped out. My back is all wet despite the air-con. I pull out the pot of yellow chrysanthemums in the trunk, but Kuya Jinny grabs them from me. Mommy reaches for my hand and we follow behind Ate Wen.

Everywhere around us are long green blankets of grass with narrow gray cement paths. We take a cemented path first, and after a while we start walking on the grass. Ate Wen treads carefully, trying not to get her pumps soiled. I remember last year it was raining, and it was muddy. Today there's no rain, but the ground is somewhat soft and wet. I try not to step on the white slabs. They are all lined up in neat rows and decorated with flowers. The dead sleep under them. I'd rather get my rubber shoes dirty.

We reach Daddy and Kuya Jinny as they settle the white pot of yellow flowers on a corner of Kuya Miguel's grave. Nana Luz had scrubbed and cleaned the slab and cut the grass around it yesterday. Ate Wen could have asked Nana Luz about the traffic.

"Sabrina," Daddy says. They have formed a line in front of me, facing Kuya Miguel's grave. I only see their backs, Daddy's like a huge mountain next to Mommy like a hill. Ate Wen and Kuya Jinny stand like tall, slim towers; Ate Wen beside Daddy, and Kuya Jinny beside Mommy.

With one jerk, Kuya Jinny pulls me to his side. Then I realize Daddy was calling me. He never calls me *Bing* like everybody else. I try to sneak a look at Daddy, but then everyone makes the sign of the cross, so I do too as fast as I can. Daddy starts praying the "Our Father" in a low speeding grumble. Kuya Jinny follows in a clearer voice, and when I peep at him, I am surprised to see his eyes closed and his whole face serious. His eyelashes are wet.

Everyone says "Amen." Daddy says, "Let's pray for our own intentions."

Slowly, I clasp my hands together. In my mind I talk to Kuya Miguel, like I do when I pray to Jesus. "Kuya Miguel, I

Saints and Souls

also want to be Kuya Jinny's buddy."

I hope it's really him when I hear in my mind, "Sure, Bing-Bang. You got it, dudette!"

∽ ∾

While Kuya Jinny and I sit in the den watching The X-Men on VHS, we hear Ate Wen's shoes tapping down the stairs. "I'm eating dinner out and that's that!" she yells.

"Rowena," Mommy calls from the landing. "It's one of the few times the family is complete—"

"We were already more complete than you could ask for at the cemetery. That's enough for the family, okay?"

"Why don't you just ask Manny to eat dinner with us here?"

"I told you, it would just make him uncomfortable. Can't you just let me go, please? I've already gone to the cemetery even if it gave me the creeps. You can eat without me, can't you?"

"Rowena." Daddy's voice booms from the living room. "That's no way to talk to your mother."

"Well, she doesn't listen. I've explained things to her over and over again. It is just a simple thing to let me go out and have dinner. I'm not staying out late or anything. Why do I have to stay locked up in this house all the time?"

"Because it's also a simple thing to ask you to stay."

Daddy has walked to the foot of the stairs. His voice sounds closer, just outside the door. "Invite your friends over. Do this for your mother." I look at Kuya Jinny watching the X-Men discuss what they have to do. He doesn't look back at me.

"I'm not a prisoner." Ate Wen's voice is final. "I'm going."

"You are NOT!" We hear a loud clapping sound. The doorknob rattles. Then the TV bursts with sounds the X-Men make, blasting against a thundering Magneto.

Finally, we hear Mommy say, "Rowena …"

The door shudders as if somebody has been leaning on it. We hear a muffled sob. "I hate this family. You're all crazy! And it's all because of Miguel's death. You want us all to suffer for it."

"Rowena, no—"

Footsteps run upstairs, and then from far away, a door slams.

"Let's watch this another time, Bing," Kuya Jinny says quietly. "I gotta do my homework."

༄ ༄

Nana Luz is in the kitchen, cutting up the vegetables. She has white hair on top of her head and many, many wrinkles going up and down her dark brown face. But when she talks, I forget she's old because she laughs all the time.

"Nana Luz, how old are you?" I ask her.

Nana Luz laughs with her mouth open and I see that she has taken off her teeth. She crouches to face me. "Why do you want to know, ha?"

I shrug. Then I hold her lips together and look straight into her crinkly laughing eyes. "I'll guess! You're ninety?"

"Ahay, hu-hu-hu," she laughs. "Too old, Ineng, I'm just sixty-three."

It's still old. Mommy once told me that Nana Luz's parents died during World War II. After that, Daddy's family adopted her and she was assigned to take care of all the babies. I'm her last baby, so I hug her. Even Daddy likes her, I know. Daddy sometimes gives her a bottle of beer, and after she drinks it, she turns red.

"Daddy slapped Ate Wen," I tell her.

"I know." Nana Luz drags the kitchen stool out for me to sit on. Then she starts cutting the string beans. "But you must not think your Daddy is bad. He's just upset."

"Why?" I ask, not sure I believe her. Daddy is the one who upsets other people.

"I think maybe he wants your family together tonight."

"But Ate Wen is right, she already went to the cemetery with us."

"You were thinking about the dead then, now is the time

to celebrate the living." She puts cooking oil on the heated pan. It hisses and sputters like something coming to life.

"He should just let Ate Wen go out with Manny."

"Pshh, you have to be more understanding. Your Ate Wen, she thinks only about herself, and forgets your Mommy needs her family now. It was hard for her when she lost the Baby Miguel."

"Baby? Nana Luz, Kuya Miguel is big now. He is my Kuya, older than me!"

"But he died when he was very small." Nana Luz holds out her dry and gnarled hands, the space between them wide enough for a basketball. "That's how I remember him."

"How did he look like?"

"Ah, very guapo, mestizo, very fair like all of you. A little prince." Nana Luz shakes her head sadly. "But he didn't live very long. Your Ate Wen, she was only two then, and kept asking to be held and carried, and your Mommy could not hold her for a long, long time. It was the trauma."

I don't really understand what *trauma* means.

Nana Luz has shut her eyes. "Your Daddy and Mommy drove very fast to get your Ate Wen home. She wanted her milk and there was no more in the car and she was crying. Hay naku, when your Ate Wen cried—"

"So it was Ate Wen's fault."

Saints and Souls

"Don't talk like that!" Nana Luz protests. "It was an accident. The truck driver was a bully and turned the corner too fast. Your Mommy was rushed to the hospital, and Baby Miguel had to be born even if it wasn't time yet. He never got out of that incubator." She explains what an incubator is, a small box in the hospital to help babies breathe. Nana Luz tells me there were many of them in the same room.

I think that means there were other babies too, who came out of their mommies' stomachs too soon, and some of them got well. But Kuya Miguel stopped breathing, so they put him in another box and buried him under the white slab, with his name written on it.

ଽ ଼

Nobody talks around the dinner table. Daddy cuts up the fried chicken, putting its butt on Mommy's plate. We all know it is her favorite part, but tonight she does not make a joke about the chicken poot-poot. In front of Mommy, and to Daddy's left, Ate Wen stares at her half-filled plate, picking at the rice but not eating it. She does not even look at her drumstick. Kuya Jinny slices up the chicken thighs on his plate and drowns the pieces in ketchup. We often fight over the other drumstick, but this time, he just lets Daddy put it on my plate without a quarrel. I try to eat properly, using my fingers, so I don't make a lot of noise with my spoon and fork sliding on the plate.

Beside me, Mommy sighs. "It's good we're all together." She looks at Ate Wen, her face kind. I think she wants to say she is sorry. I want to tell her to hold Ate Wen.

Ate Wen concentrates on piercing a string bean slowly with her fork. She does not look at any of us. Her eyes are thick and gummy and red.

"Eat up, Rowena," Daddy commands, but his voice does not boom. He rests his huge hand on Ate Wen's shoulder. "What's wrong with Sabrina over there?" Daddy suddenly asks. "She looks so stiff."

I feel all of them looking at me. I take a few bites of chicken and fill my mouth up with rice.

"Well, at least one of us is eating well," Daddy laughs. Nobody laughs with him.

Suddenly I have an idea. And before I can stop to think more about it, I find myself already talking. "Daddy, we can transfer Kuya Miguel to our backyard."

Mommy and Daddy both look up. They seem puzzled, and suddenly I feel uncertain.

"What do you mean? Always say what you mean, Sabrina."

Saints and Souls

I swallow. "We can put him in our backyard with his name tag. So we can visit him on November 1 and there won't be traffic." I don't know what else to do, so I sit on my hands.

All at once, the room fills up with Daddy's laughter. Mommy's face breaks into a smile, and for a while she looks almost happy.

"Your sister...," Daddy tells Ate Wen. "She wants Miguel's grave out in the backyard."

"She's—she's funny," Ate Wen says, as if she's not sure. She sweeps her fingers lightly up over her face, over her eyes and forehead and down her hair. Did she hear me at all the first time?

Kuya Jinny looks puzzled too. When he sees me looking, he crosses his eyes at me. Don't they want to visit Kuya Miguel on November 1 so that he could be a saint too, like many Filipinos? So that we could follow tradition?

"Aww, Bing, don't look so confused. That was a ... a thoughtful idea." Mommy puts an arm around me, laughing and wiping her eyes. "Look at her face!" she tells the others.

"You can't just dig up a grave and bring it here, Bing," Kuya Jinny explains.

"Why not?"

"Well ... well, because the priests have to give permission," Kuya Jinny answers, and everyone laughs some more.

I want to laugh too. "When we die," I tell them, "if we have to stay in the cemetery, our family will visit us on November 2, and we'll all be souls." At least we'll be souls together.

"Bing!" Mommy protests, and she looks a bit shocked.

Daddy staggers up, laughing loudly. "Why, Sabrina, YOU are the family clown." He leans over my chair to give me a hug and mess up my hair.

∽ ∾

When Ate Wen turns off all the lights, I curl up in my bed with my blanket wrapped around me. I make sure my face sticks out. I pretend I am inside an incubator, breathing fine.

"Goodnight, Bing." Ate Wen's voice peals like little bells in the dark.

I am too surprised to answer her. Ate Wen never says goodnight to me. We keep quiet once the light is turned off, and fall asleep. Most of the time, I fall asleep even before she even comes into the room. Ate Wen can stay up as late as she wants.

Ate Wen is very pretty. Small and like a princess. Her voice, when she speaks, sounds beautiful and clear, even when she's angry. And she looks serious all the time, just like Daddy. Maybe that's why Nana Luz says she's Daddy's favorite, even if Kuya Jinny looks more like him. They say I look like Mommy most.

In my arms, I am holding a baby. Sometimes the baby looks like Ate Wen, sometimes like Kuya Jinny. I want to make the baby laugh, really laugh, from the very insides of its soul.

Trouble and Tears

for David and Diego

The children were surprised when Mama mysteriously disappeared one summer evening. They waited past supper, and they waited until bedtime. And then Lola tucked them in their beds, told them a story about a kindhearted girl who looked up the sky and saw heaven, and said, "Don't worry, she'll be here in the morning."

Sib still did not want to go to sleep, so she said, "But why did the girl see heaven, Lola?"

"Because she was kindhearted."

"What did she do to be kindhearted?"

"She gave her old clothes to the poor, she gave them food, she talked to them … and brought medicine when they were sick, and … and if you're a good girl, you may one day look up at the sky and see heaven yourself."

Cecilia was more interested in heaven than in being good. "What did it look like, Lola? When the clouds parted, what did the girl see?"

"She saw a palace, a beautiful garden, lots of fountains, angels walking and talking and—"

"Singing, of course!" Meren cried.

"Angels!" Cecilia cried.

"Fountains!" Sib cried.

"Of course," Lola laughed, and then kissed their foreheads. "Now go to sleep, girls, and in the morning, Mama will be here."

In the dark, Meren, being the eldest, called to her sisters. "Is anyone afraid? Are you worried about Mama?"

But Sib, being the youngest, was already asleep, and Cecilia only said, "I hope she brings home a surprise," before she turned over and snored.

Meren lay in the dark, wondering about Mama for a while, then thought of Mama looking up at the sky and seeing the angels singing. She smiled to herself—didn't Lola tell such wonderful stories! And Meren, at last, drifted off to sleep.

୭ ୨

The next morning, the three girls raced to the kitchen, then to the dining room, and without bothering about kissing Lola, and eating their breakfast, they rushed on to the living room and out the front door. There was no sign of Mama, or her car.

Trouble and Tears

"Where is she?" Sib wailed, and Meren had to comfort her.

Cecilia went down the front steps and onto the curb, looking up and down the street. And then she pointed at the yellow flowers growing in a pot beside their door. "Mama would like those."

Lola had followed them, and said, "Yes, she would, and she would also like you to have breakfast."

They were about to follow Lola in when they heard a car coming down the road, its horn tooting three times.

"Mama!" Sib cried, and there she was behind the wheel, waving and grinning at them, like she had a big secret. Behind her, there was a curly-haired woman they had not seen before. Mama got out of her car and then opened the back door to let the woman out. The curly-haired woman bent, and brought out something in a bundle. Mama also brought out another. Something under the blanket began to squirm.

"Puppies!" Cecilia clapped her hands, and then her hands went to her mouth, because a cry came out of the bundle. It did not sound like a puppy at all. The girls ran to surround Mama, and she had to sit on her heels for them to see what was inside, wrapped in the blanket.

"Oh," they said, and then peered at the other bundle, which the curly-haired woman had placed on Mama's other arm. "Ah!"

"Twins?" Meren guessed, and when Mama nodded, she felt so pleased with her intelligence. "Are they boys or girls?" she asked.

"Boys," Mama answered, and announced, "they will be your brothers."

And the three girls could not believe what they heard, so they started clapping and singing and dancing. They looked like angels themselves.

"We're adopting them," they heard Mama tell Lola.

And Lola said, in a tone that the girls had never heard before, "But where did they come from? What do we know of their parents? You are still of child-bearing age. Isn't blood thicker than water?"

The girls stopped. They looked at their Lola as if they thought she was going to tell a story. They did not understand what she had said.

"It's very kindhearted of Mama," Meren offered.

But Lola only shook her head, and walked back into the house, leaving them all behind.

∽ ∾

"Since you are now grown-up, these two are my new babies, and you as older sisters will help me take care of them." On each arm, Mama carried a baby.

The girls gathered around her on the bed. Sib squeezed past her elder sisters and lay her head upon Mama's tummy. "Can't I be a baby too?" she asked. "Sometimes?" But they all just laughed at her.

Trouble and Tears

"You're an Ate now, silly," Cecilia said beside her, then turned to Mama. "Where did you find them? Did you go to the hospital?"

So then Mama told them a story, about a young girl who gave birth to twins but could not take care of them because she was so poor. And she looked up at the sky and prayed, "Oh Lord, please send me a mother for these two."

"Why, if she's poor? Why couldn't she take care of them?" Sib asked.

Mama sighed. "She did not have money to buy their milk and their diapers. She had no one to help her."

"And then? And then how did you hear?" Meren asked, thinking again of the opening sky, of heaven, of the angels talking directly to Mama and telling her to go and help the poor girl with the two babies.

"A doctor heard the poor girl as she prayed, and the doctor told me, and I thought that you would like brothers. Would you?"

"Oh yes," cried Cecilia, clapping her hands.

"Yes," Meren nodded, beaming at her kindhearted mother.

"They're ours," cried Sib, throwing her small arms around each one. "Our brothers."

And then Lola walked into the room, looked at the two bundles, and said, "But they don't look like you at all."

The twins, each wrapped in a baby blanket, Mama called her bundles of joy. "Jorge," she said into the telephone, "come home soon and see our bundles of joy!"

And Lola clucked at the three sisters and said, "Maybe Jorge will call them bundles of sorrow."

Cecilia was more interested in what to call them rather than in sorrow. She was tired of referring to them as Mama's bundles of joy.

"Francis and Anthony, of course," Meren said, hugging herself for her cleverness, for were not Francis and Anthony Papa's favorite saints?

"No, no, Derek and Dylan," Cecilia said, using the names Papa had picked for her puppies, if Santa Claus would one day give her puppies.

And Sib looked at one twin, and then the other, and said, "How will we know who is who?"

"This one is Tears," pointed Lola, "and this one is Trouble."

And Mama suddenly stood up from her seat and gave one twin to Meren, and the other to Cecilia. And when Sib demanded that she wanted one too, Mama grabbed her hand and said, "No Sib, you help me with bathing them, while your Ates hold them. Let's go girls." And everybody followed without looking at Lola, who was left behind.

ร ∾

Trouble and Tears

Sib took delight in being Mama's number one helper. Mama taught her how to pour the water slowly from the tabo, while Mama gently washed one baby's head, and soaped his body, then quickly gave the baby to Meren or Cecilia, who waited to catch the baby in a towel. The twin whom Lola had named Tears, indeed cried a lot of the time, and Trouble kept on soiling his diapers.

Sib watched as Tears' face turned red, and his nose scrunched up, and his mouth rounded into an angry roar. Sib watched as Trouble kicked, then stretched his legs, then opened his eyes wide as his diaper grew heavy. Then Sib looked at Mama, who laughed and never looked angry, except when Lola came into the room and shook her head. And Sib then looked at Lola, who looked solemnly back at her, and sighed.

One day, Sib overheard Lola in the kitchen, telling a story to the curly-haired woman, who was named Yaya Ising, and who, after Mama went back to work, would help the three sisters take care of the twins.

"I have blood that comes from seven nationalities," Lola said. "Spanish, German, French, British, American, Filipino, and Chinese. My father was a very decent gentleman who owned land, and my mother came from a family of doctors, shipowners, and educators."

"Oh," Yaya Ising said. She was washing several milk bottles.

"Those boys. Where could they have come from? What is in their blood?"

Sib told her sisters about the blood at once. The three of them went to look at Tears and Trouble in the crib they shared, bootie to bootie, where they lay sleeping. Tears smiled, his tiny eyelids shut more tightly for a second, before relaxing into sleep again. Trouble's arms waved, a hand inside the mitten opened and closed, and they heard him sigh softly.

"I don't want them ever to bleed," whispered Meren.

Cecilia nodded. "We must always watch them, and catch them if they fall from their bicycles."

And Sib said, "Lola must never look at their blood."

႒ ႒

Towards the end of summer, Papa came home. He had spent the summer in China, teaching English at a university in Beijing. He had many stories to tell his three girls, but so did they, and he had to let them tell theirs first.

"Tears loves to think," Meren said. "He looks into your eyes, or far away, out the window, and he stares and stares and thinks."

"And Trouble loves to talk," Cecilia said. "He makes gurgling noises, and bubbles come out of his mouth, and sometimes, he hiccups."

"But Tears and Trouble both love Mama's rocking chair," Sib said. "They fall asleep quickly when they're there. And they love being sung to, I sing 'Rock-a-bye' to them."

Trouble and Tears

Lola looked at the three girls, all so eager to tell their stories. They had forgotten all about hers.

"Jorge," Mama said, taking his arm, "we really have to think of names for them."

"Oh, I don't know," Papa laughed, "Tears and Trouble seem to be just fine." And Lola smirked.

"Jorge," Mama cried. "Be serious."

And then they heard, coming from afar, coming from upstairs, the sound of a baby crying. The girls rushed to the rescue at once, and Mama and Papa followed. Lola, shrugging and shaking her head, and following much more slowly, brought up the rear.

Immediately there were bursts of giggling, and shrieks of laughter from the girls. Everyone looked inside the crib. Tears was crying, kicking furiously, his mittens scrunched up into tight fists, and he had no diaper on. Trouble was gurgling, kicking as well, and waving a diaper at them.

The girls laughed; they couldn't stop. Mama laughed as she took Tears and placed him in Papa's arms, then tried to take the diaper from Trouble. Papa laughed at the little tug-of-war, then laughed when Trouble gave up the diaper and crooned, then laughed some more, choking, when Tears stuck a mittened hand into his mouth. And Lola laughed a little before sighing and raising her eyes to heaven.

As Mama and Papa tucked them in their beds that night, they wondered again about what to call Tears and Trouble.

"Anthony and Francis?" Meren offered.

"Dylan and Derek?" Cecilia suggested.

And Sib just kept quiet, watching Lola at the door.

Papa kissed them on their foreheads. "We will all sleep on it, and tomorrow morning, their names will come."

In the dark, Sib, unable to sleep, called to her sisters. "Are you thinking of names?"

But Meren only mumbled, and Cecilia was already snoring. Sib lay for a moment, looking up at the ceiling, then wondered if the ceiling would open, and then the clouds. She thought of the angels waving at her, at her sisters; she thought of angels making Tears and Trouble smile in their sleep. And then she thought of Lola.

That night, Sib did not sleep in her bed, but between Papa and Mama. She whispered in her Mama's ear, "I'm your baby still, sometimes," and in her Papa's, "You have to think of Lola's seven bloods." And then she fell asleep.

The next morning, Sib woke in her bed, and heard her two older sisters getting dressed for the day. "Wait," she cried, and Meren and Cecilia dressed her up quickly. The three girls raced to the kitchen, then to the dining room, and found Papa and Lola eating their breakfast at one end of the table. At the other end of the table, Mama and Yaya Ising each carried a twin and held a bottle to his mouth.

"Names!" they demanded, but Papa told them to have breakfast first. They chomped their tapa, they chewed their fried rice, they swallowed their milk, from time to time spotting a little mitten or a little bootie waving.

And when they were finished, they turned eagerly in their seats to face Papa. Papa stood, took Tears from Mama's arms, then said, "This guy we will name after Lola's brother, Ernesto," and he offered the baby to Lola, who accepted him. Papa then took Trouble from Yaya Ising's arms, and said, "And this guy we will name after Lola's father, Eugenio," and he gave the other baby to Lola as well.

Mama watched, the three girls watched, as Lola looked from one twin to the other. "I will tell them stories of Ernesto and Eugenio one day," Lola said softly, and she looked up and smiled. Ernesto began to wail, and Eugenio began to wave. And Lola laughed.

"Ernesto and Eugenio," Meren said.

"Eugenio and Ernesto," Cecilia said.

"Tears and Trouble, Trouble and Tears," Sib whispered, looking at Lola, then smiled and added, "No more, no more."

The Skylab

Marty pushed past the school guards. He glanced at his wrist, felt shock, and then calmed down. He remembered that Ton-Ton would be wearing his Mickey Mouse watch for a week in exchange for reading Ton-Ton's *Casper* and *Spooky* comics. He did not realize it would be so hard to keep track of the time without a watch. "It's only 7:10," his father had said, just before Marty left the Toyota. His father had placed his huge hand on Marty's head. "Why don't you just enjoy your school days without worrying so much about time?"

But he was worried, because he never liked missing frog ceremony. It was the highlight of his and Ton-Ton's morning, watching the girls in grade four scream and leap out of the line whenever a frog's webbed foot got caught in the lace of Amy's socks. The sound of Amy's shrieks would drown out the scratchy sound of *Lupang Hinirang* issuing forth from the loudspeakers. She would scream until the end of the morning prayer.

As usual, there was already a roaring noise of high school students on the quadrangle, harder to group and force into lines. But as Marty cleared the crowd, he saw that the grade school students had not formed their own lines either. Most of them stood at random, in little clumps of three or five, all looking up at the sky. Marty stopped in his tracks and looked up too, but there was nothing there but the white July sky, and a few loose clouds. Wonderingly, he looked for Ton-Ton.

"They should just make today a holiday," Ton-Ton was declaring to Jamil, and to anybody else who would listen.

"Yeah," agreed Jamil. "They just want to torture us, even if it is the last day of the world."

Just as Jamil said that, the sky shadowed for a moment and put a chill in Marty's stomach. He suddenly felt like going to the bathroom. "Hey, what's up?" Marty asked, his voice squeaking a bit. He hoped nobody would think he was afraid; he did not even know what was going on yet.

"Oh the world will probably end today," Ton-Ton answered, quite happily, like he was going to have a birthday party. "The Skylab is falling."

"The Skylab?"

"You know," Ton-Ton prompted, like Marty was the dumbest guy on earth, "that satellite in the sky that lost its orbit. It's falling right this minute." Ton-Ton's left hand resembled a UFO falling from the sky, rushing to smack onto his other hand. The silver of Marty's watch, right at the tail

The Skylab

end of the UFO, glinted in the daylight. "If it hits the Philippines," Ton-Ton added, "it will sink us all." His right hand lowered visibly.

"Oh, *that* Skylab," Marty nodded, imagining a big, round, and monstrous spaceship with metal tentacles.

"It's as big as the earth," Jamil contributed. "It'll knock us all into the sun, and we'll burn like we're in hell."

"HOOO!" hooted Ton-Ton derisively. "They built it in the States, dummy, it can't be as big as Earth too. It's really just as big as the Philippines, which is twenty times smaller than the USA."

Marty listened to Ton-Ton, half-skeptical and half-impressed. Ton-Ton loved to make up a lot of stuff, but when it came to geography and history, he was a whiz. All the Social Studies teachers liked him, even when sometimes he purposely wrote the wrong answers to test questions or made up his own current events. Their present Social Studies teacher, Mr Marquez, had even worked with Ton-Ton to provide silly answers to questions they already knew the answers to. Who is the national hero of the Philippines? –Uncle Sam. Who is the President of the Philippines? –Mekanda Robot. What is the national bird? –Batman and Robin. "You can be president after Mekanda, Ton-Ton," Mr Marquez would say. But if the Skylab killed them, Ton-Ton would not even get the chance to be president. Ton-Ton would not be able to declare watching Japanese robot cartoons as part of their subjects in school.

Marty frowned, getting into the spirit of rebellion. "They should cancel classes. We might as well have fun on our last day."

Nearby, Ella was sobbing. "I want to go home. We shouldn't be here."

"School really wants to take all the fun away," Cris complained.

"Don't worry," Amy crooned, trying to comfort one and appease the other. "At least we're all still together."

"All right, Section 2, form your lines for flag ceremony," called Mrs Perez, their homeroom teacher, waddling her way, to the left, and to the right, and around Marty's classmates. "Stop that!" she scolded Ella, fishing out a tissue from one of the huge pockets of her dress. Marty was about to obey when he noticed Ton-Ton had not moved, and was again looking up at the sky.

"I thought I saw something," Ton-Ton whispered, shielding his eyes from the sun. Again the Mickey Mouse wristwatch flashed on Ton-Ton's white wrist.

Mrs Perez reached them. "Antonio de Leon, Martin Encarnacion, get to your places."

But Ton-Ton still continued to scan the skies, and Marty followed suit. What if somewhere in Japan Voltes V, Mazinger Z, and Daimos did exist? What if they were top secret, but now was the time for them to fly into view, to stop the Skylab from falling?

The skylab

He felt a sudden twisting pain in his upper arm where Mrs Perez grabbed him. "Get to your places, I said," she cried, dragging both Ton-Ton and him to the Section 2 line.

"Ow, Mrs Perez," Ton-Ton protested, his dark eyes glaring. "Won't you be kind to us now, this is your last chance to be good."

∽ ∾

The silence that filled the classroom ate at the edges of Marty's stomach. He wanted to raise his hand and ask to be excused, but he was sure that that would only make his classmates stiffen instead of laugh at his daring. So he clamped his mouth shut and waited for his execution. He only hoped it would come before he dropped his stinkbomb on all of them.

Mrs Perez grabbed Ton-Ton's collar to hurry him to her desk, and waited for Marty to follow behind. At least Marty would be able to see what form his execution would take, because Ton-Ton was to go first. Mrs Perez opened her table drawer. It was full of plastic rulers, the kind that one could buy at the canteen. They looked almost like red and green, orange and yellow jelly—even the blue one could have been jelly—but when they landed and broke on Ton-Ton's hand, they sounded too hard to be jelly. Three, four, five, Marty counted, trying to harden his stomach. Eight, nine, ten, but something sharp, the pointy part of his heart, maybe, was trying to puncture it.

"This will teach you to listen next time," Mrs Perez roared. "Next time, clean your ears. Next time, listen and obey!"

Ton-Ton laughed. He was just as red as Mrs Perez, and his cheeks were wet, although there were no tears in his eyes. The blue ruler descended upon Ton-Ton's hand three times before it broke. As soon as he caught his breath, he said, "But Mrs Perez, there won't be a next time."

Mrs Perez simply pushed him aside and signed for Marty. If he could not have his holiday, Marty thought, extending his hand, it would not be so bad if the Skylab fell just about now. He waited. But everything crashed on his hand and not on his head. He tried not to look at the silent classmates around him, who were watching, he knew, with curiosity. None would blame him or Ton-Ton, but none would feel sympathy for them either. None would think Mrs Perez unfair. He tried not to look at Amy as he took his seat between hers and the window. But then when he finally made a quick scan of the room, he saw that his classmates still faced forward, watching Mrs Perez sweep the pile of broken rulers into the wastebasket.

Ton-Ton, who sat in front of Marty, was the only one not looking. He was looking up at the sky again. "Psst, Ton, do you see anything?"

"Before SHE interrupted us, I did. I thought it was the Skylab. It was something metallic."

"What if that were a robot from Japan?"

The Skylab

"Those aren't real," Ton-Ton scoffed, then straightened up when he saw Mrs Perez rise from behind her desk. He looked out the window again, ignoring her glare.

Marty feared she would punish them again, so he looked down at the scratched wood of his desk and tried to look well-behaved. With a finger, he traced the words carved into the desk—Missing, VV, Sarah loves Lo-, Toyota vs Crispa. He wanted to add his name to the wood, although he had never felt the temptation to before. And then he felt a tingle rise from the bottom of his spine. Tomorrow, would his desk be there at all?

"Well," Mrs Perez finally called into the quiet. She gave a short nod and turned to go, not looking at either Ton-Ton or Marty. "See you in Math class. Sixth period." It took her forever to lumber to the door at the back and leave the room. The moment she took a step out, several of the boys ran to the wastebasket to peer at the rulers.

"Pssh," Ton-Ton told them from his seat. "It didn't hurt one bit, right Marty?"

"No way," Marty shook his head. To convince Ton-Ton, he started carving out both their names on his desk with a ballpen, using both his smarting hands. Ton-Ton and Marty. Someday, their names would float out from the bottom of the sea.

∽ ∾

57

"My mommy got a call from Mindanao this morning," Cris said. "It was her auntie telling her not to leave the house and to put black cloth over all of the windows. She's crazy." She was talking to Amy, Marcia, and Ella, but she was looking at Ton-Ton. Marty watched as Ton-Ton ignored her, taking another big bite of his Spam sandwich.

Ella shook her head. "What if the auntie is right? How do we know she is not?"

"What a worrier," Cris commented.

"But she could be right," Ella wailed, shivering. "My grandmother says we should not even open the door to anyone who knocks, because if we do, it would turn out to be the devil."

"So what are you doing in school?" Marcia asked pointedly.

Then Ton-Ton yelled. "It's coming, it's coming, aaahhh!" He fell dramatically to the floor as if he had just been hit from above. The girls began screaming and crouching low, their hands on their heads. Marty, shocked at first, then catching on to Ton-Ton's game, burst into laughter.

Both Ton-Ton and Marty received a few punches and pinches from Amy and Marcia. Ella started crying in earnest. "You stupids," cried Cris, genuinely furious, giving the most pain with her kicks. "You ought to be punished, shot, murdered in your seats." Marty tried to ward her off, then was surprised to see Ton-Ton still on the floor, slapping at Cris' flying feet half-heartedly. He was looking out the window. He looked a

The Skylab

bit pale, and his shirt was dirty. The watch glinted, blinding Marty momentarily.

Ton-Ton blinked. "We should not have classes. This is wrong. I'm going to tell Mr Marquez." He stood up.

"Don't," Marty cried, placing a hand on his arm. "Are you crazy? We're not supposed to go to the Faculty Room unless we're asked to."

"Pshh," Ton-Ton replied, snatching his arm away, "who cares about rules now?"

After hesitating a while, the girls followed Ton-Ton out of the classroom and down two flights of stairs. Jamil was at Ton-Ton's elbow, keeping up with Ton-Ton's strides at the same time he told every grade four student the plan. Marty brought up the rear, opening and closing his hands. They still smarted from the blows Mrs Perez had given them. In the pit of his stomach, he knew this was the wrong idea, but he felt he had no other alternative. He did just want to go home and read at least one more *Spooky* comic, and watch one more robot cartoon.

At the door of the Faculty Room, Ton-Ton paused and turned to face his followers. Most of Section 2 and some of Section 1 and 3 had joined them. Ton-Ton winked and banged on the door. The door opened so quickly that some people in front staggered forward, while the ones behind ran away in fright. Marty forced his feet to stay where they were.

"Hello, Ton-Ton, what can I do for you?" Miss Fonacier's voice wafted around them, before Marty found the courage to look. Miss Fonacier had been their grade three Social Studies teacher. She had also been particularly impressed with Ton-Ton. Marty's heart slowed down and stopped jabbing into his stomach.

"Miss Fonacier," Ton-Ton began, "we all have to leave school now—"

"Leave school?" Miss Fonacier's voice rose an octave. She looked behind her, stepped out, and shut the door. She took Ton-Ton's elbow, and led him, and therefore the crowd, to one of the benches against the long wall of the Faculty Room. "Why?" she asked.

"We're not supposed to be here, because the Skylab is falling and we deserve a holiday," Ton-Ton explained.

Miss Fonacier laughed, and everybody smiled around her. Marty found himself smiling too. "Phew, don't we all deserve a holiday. But—"

"Hey, what's up? Is this a rally or what?" It was Mr Marquez, a chalkbox in one hand, and a folded map and roll of masking tape in the other. He was probably on his way to Section 2. The bell was about to ring.

"They want a holiday because of the Skylab," Miss Fonacier informed him.

"It's the end of the world," Ella fretted.

The Skylab

"Is it?" Miss Fonacier asked, still smiling.

Mr Marquez groaned. "Are you a Seventh-Day Adventist by any chance, Ella?"

Miss Fonacier laughed. "Lito—"

Mr Marquez fell on his knees and gestured to Miss Fonacier. " 'Had we but world enough and time,' my lady." Then the bell rang. Everyone groaned. Mr Marquez rose quickly to his feet, dusting his knee. "So much for time. Let's go, my people, there is much to be discussed. Onward march!" Then he turned around to see if everyone followed. "Sections 1 and 3, please go back to your rooms. Wait for your Social Studies period, okay? We'll talk about the Skylab. Mr President, if you would please not get yourself late."

Ton-Ton had remained standing beside Miss Fonacier. After waving at Mr Marquez, he knelt in mock imitation. "Miss Fonacier, you are the greatest, prettiest teacher. Thank you!"

Yet again, Miss Fonacier laughed. "You really would make a great politician, Mr de Leon. Thank you for the compliment. Now go to class and behave yourself so that the history books will give you a sparkling review."

Ton-Ton and Marty watched Miss Fonacier disappear into the Faculty Room before they walked back to the stairs. On the landing, Ton-Ton paused once to look up at the sky, sighing.

∽ ∾

Mr Marquez was waiting for them. "Everyone stand to attention, the President is here." He never tired playing his game, but the others groaned and mumbled in their seats. "I heard about your trial by fire, Ton-Ton, and Marty too. Mrs Perez told all the faculty herself ten thousand times." Marty clutched at his hands to check if the smarting was still there. It was not. "You know it does not pay to talk back to a teacher."

Ton-Ton simply grinned back at him. "It's never good to talk back to the future president either."

"Will you decree the Skylab to fall on her head?"

Ton-Ton frowned. "When will it land?" he asked Mr Marquez.

Mr Marquez looked around his class and then smiled at Marty. "Don't look so worried, Mart. Everyone, listen. The Skylab will probably land in Australia." He pointed to a large pink spot towards the bottom of the world map already taped to the board. Marty heard sighs of relief all around him.

"And what will happen to the Australians?" Ella asked, raising her hand but not waiting to be called. "Will they all drown?"

Mr Marquez smiled at her. "You sure have a doomsday view of the world, Ella." He looked around him. "It's not yet the end of the world today, I assure you. Now don't be too disappointed. In space, the Skylab will break into thousands of pieces, and those pieces will hit the ground. Some will be as huge as cars and trucks, but nothing so big as to sink a whole country."

"Why is it falling?" Amy asked.

"Something went wrong with the satellite. Those American products go wrong too, you know. Your Mickey Mouse watch will get broken too, someday, Ton-Ton."

Ton-Ton winked at Marty, not correcting Mr Marquez.

"So," Mr Marquez said, hand poised with chalk upon the blackboard, "back to the voting, like the last time. Who would still like the Philippines to be a colony—remember that word, 'colony'?—a province of the United States?"

Marty did not raise his hand with half the class. He wanted to be Japanese, so he could watch a lot of their robot cartoons. He remembered telling Ton-Ton this, and Ton-Ton had teased him about it, saying it was because Marty looked Japanese.

"Ton-Ton, why are you raising your hand? Have you given up your ambition, or are you planning to be President of the US as well?"

"I just want to have snow," Ton-Ton answered readily, making everyone laugh, because they had just learned about the equator and the tropics in Science. But then he continued, in a voice full of wishes, "I want to feel the cold, roll in the ground, hide out in the snow."

When Mrs Perez entered the classroom, there was a gigantic hush. But Ton-Ton beamed diplomatically and extended his left hand to Mrs Perez. "Sorry about my behavior, Mrs Perez. I thought it was the end of the world."

Mrs Perez looked at the hand, then at the watch. "You'll have to prove your sincerity with good manners, Antonio," Mrs Perez said solemnly, but she took his hand.

"Mr Marquez said not to worry, the Skylab will just fall in Australia, where they'll be able to handle the situation better. Thank God it won't happen here."

"Pssh, run along now, back to your desk. You just parrot whatever your hero Mr Marquez says."

Marty sat among his classmates, unable to move. Mrs Perez did not look at him, but he felt that she was waiting, and the class was waiting. Marty stared at the watch on Ton-Ton's hand, the watch that was beginning to look more and more like Ton-Ton owned it. If Marty had been wearing the watch, then he would have been just as brave as Ton-Ton. It was the watch.

"Now, Ton-Ton, Jamil, please pick up the new Math workbooks at the Faculty Room." Both Ton-Ton and Jamil left quickly. Marty sat, stunned. Everybody knew that he and Ton-Ton were partners, and that they always did things together. Could Mrs Perez be so cruel? Was she punishing him for not apologizing? Were not the rulers enough?

Mrs Perez turned back to the class. "You know, Mr Marquez doesn't know everything. And not everything he says

The Skylab

might be true. Did he ever say our President loves children a lot? He has given many schools new textbooks. If you watch channel 4, you will see him and the First Lady surrounded by children." Marty could hardly listen. By the time Ton-Ton and Jamil came back, he was blinking at the blackboard, at the page numbers that Mrs Perez had written there. Ton-Ton handed him a workbook. Marty flipped to one of the pages absently. "What are we supposed to do?" he whispered.

"Look at your page. What else is there? Answer the exercises. Sheesh!" Ton-Ton rolled his eyes, then went back to writing his answers on the workbook. With his left hand, the hand that seemed so big with the watch, he covered his own page.

Stung, Marty retreated to his page too. Once he got his watch back, he vowed, he would never make deals with Ton-Ton again.

"Martin Encarnacion, Antonio de Leon," shrieked Mrs Perez, right in Marty's ear. "I said DO NOT WRITE ON THOSE BOOKS! Why don't you ever listen?"

"But, but ..." Marty stammered, gesturing towards Ton-Ton. Ton-Ton was winking at him.

"You give your excuses to the principal," yelled Mrs Perez. "Go ahead, get out. Go to the principal's office right now."

In a daze, and through the utter silence in class, Marty stumbled after Ton-Ton outside. Ton-Ton was skipping. "We're free, partner, free from the enemy!"

Marty struggled against the angry knots forming in his throat and took a huge gulp of air. "You planned this? You knew we weren't supposed to write on the books?" He already knew the answer.

Ton-Ton looked at him and laughed. "Don't look so worried, Mart," he said. "We'll get through this like we always do." He slapped Marty's arm. "Together."

The secretary informed them that the principal was at a meeting, so they had to wait on one of the sofas outside his door. She gave each of them a form to fill up. Name, grade, section. Sent by (teacher's name). Offense (if known). Marty's heart grew heavier and heavier, so that it once again perched at the top of his stomach. Ton-Ton, his hands and chin in the air, made a show of collecting their forms and giving them back to the secretary, trying to win her with a smile. She simply glanced at the forms before putting them aside and resuming her typing.

"You'll be my secretary, Marty," Ton-Ton said in an undertone. Marty looked at his friend, not sure how to react. He did want to be with Ton-Ton when he became president, but he was not sure he would enjoy typing. He also was not sure he liked the idea of Ton-Ton planning everything for him.

"Is that all I could be?" Marty asked him, rather angrily.

"Dummy, you could be anything you want."

He did not like being called a dummy either, but he saw that Ton-Ton had meant it, that he could be anything he

The Skylab

wanted, that Ton-Ton would not mind so much if he did not want to be secretary. The fluorescent directly above shone a light down on Ton-Ton's fair face, and formed a halo round his head. Marty felt the watch rest on his palm. "Here, Marty, you can have it back today, but you can still hang on to my comics."

"No," Marty said, handing it back. "A deal is a deal." He felt rather like a hero saying that.

The bell rang, making them jump. It sounded like a fire alarm, here in the principal's office. The secretary stood up, about to go out with her folder, when she noticed the two of them. "I almost forgot about you. You can see the principal tomorrow. Here, take these slips and show them to your teacher, so that you can come here during Homeroom period."

"Thank you," Ton-Ton said, taking the two slips and sticking them in his back pocket. He grinned at Marty. No Mrs Perez until sixth period tomorrow.

∽ ∾

Seated next to his father, in the front seat of the car, Marty looked at the darkening sky, a strange red and violet. He kept forgetting what Mr Marquez had told them that day, that there would still be life, that there would still be school tomorrow. It seemed easier somehow to believe that it was doomsday. And he found he still did not want to see the principal the next day.

"I wish I didn't have to go to school tomorrow," Ton-Ton said, as if he had listened to Marty's thoughts. Ton-Ton usually rode at the back, with Marty and his father. They dropped Ton-Ton off in Cubao where the market was.

"Thank you, Dr Encarnacion," Ton-Ton said, before slamming the door and waving at Marty.

Marty watched his friend walking away, skillfully dodging pedestrians, but looking small with his big black bag slung over one of his shoulders. It looked as if the bag had eaten half of his back. Ton-Ton's UFO hand glinted as it gripped the bag in place.

"You better get your watch back before your mommy finds out," his father spoke up, surprising Marty. He had hoped that no one in his family would notice, until he got it back the next week. His father's hand rested on Marty's head a moment, before he took it back to turn the steering wheel. "Ton-Ton is brave, isn't he? He's not scared of going home alone."

"I could do that too," Marty told him, knowing full well that his mother did not like the idea.

His father smiled, keeping his eyes on the road. "Maybe next year," he replied. "It's an exciting but dangerous world out there."

Marty wanted to speak up, to tell him that it was also exciting and dangerous in school. He wanted to tell him of the Skylab—did he know about it?—of Mrs Perez's cruelty, of Ton-Ton's deviousness. But then he thought his father would get angry about disobeying the rules. And, his father would learn about his trips to the principal all too soon.

The Skylab

When they got home, Marty changed his clothes without having to be told, and got a smile from his father before his father disappeared into his clinic adjoining the house. In the dining room, he made himself a Spam sandwich and settled down to watch *Daimos*. After the cartoon, he waited awhile to see if this would be one of the days when Ton-Ton would call to talk about an episode, but he did not. He decided not to call Ton-Ton either. Marty finally spread out his notebook on the dining table to face the math problems they had missed doing in class. He and Ton-Ton had been made to copy them from the workbooks. That Mrs Perez really thought of everything.

One more day, he told himself. One more day until the weekend. Five more days until he got his watch back. Three more weeks until his birthday. Five more months until Christmas vacation. He was in the midst of counting the days when the telephone rang. Marty raced to the living room before his father could answer the call from the extension in his clinic. "Hello?"

"Mart."

"Ton! Wasn't that a great episode of *Daimos*, huh? That new sting weapon of the enemy's was so powerful, I thought. But then Richard always wins, right?"

There was a silence at the other end that startled Marty. "Ton-Ton?"

"Hey," whispered Ton-Ton, then there was long intake of breath. "I'm not going to school tomorrow—"

"You're letting me go to the principal alone! Traitor!" The silence checked him again. Marty's stomach grew heavy. "It'll be okay, Ton-Ton, you said we'd go together," he pleaded.

"I … I have to leave school. My mom says we have to go far away. Maybe the States, that would be fun. Except … my father isn't coming. He has to stay behind. He had to go with these two men who were waiting for him when I came home. They drove off in an army jeep. It was really old-looking and dusty, and made a snorting sound. Mom say's he'll be staying with them in camp before he comes to join us. He'll follow."

"Camp," Marty repeated, but only because he did not know what else to say to this person who did not sound much like Ton-Ton.

"Mom has to use the phone now. She says goodbye to you. So … bye."

Marty stood up. He did not understand. And he almost did not hear the click at the other end. He suddenly felt the world turn. His father found him lying face down on the floor in tears, sobbing into the receiver, "You'll have snow! You'll have Mickey Mouse!" He let himself be carried to his room.

His father stayed with him until he fell asleep, clinging to his father's huge hand.

The Skylab

In the middle of the night, Marty woke up, remembering everything Mr Marquez had told them in class. About how people suddenly disappeared from their homes and no one ever found them again. He had to do something, maybe warn Ton-Ton. He crept out of his room and down the stairs. He picked up the phone and dialed Ton-Ton's number in the dark. Ton-Ton's phone rang at once, loudly, in Marty's ear. Marty listened to the ringing, until the busy signal sounded. He dialed again, and a third time, but there was no answer.

Tomorrow, he decided, he would have to ask Mr Marquez's help. Then he thought of Mr Marquez kneeling and reciting poems, cracking jokes and saying, "Don't worry, Mart." He sighed. There was no hope.

He went back to his room. As he squeezed past his door, he knocked some things off the bedside table, things that scattered and made a shuffling sound. He switched on the lamp and looked down at the *Casper* and *Spooky* comics, all that he had left of Ton-Ton. Then he thought of their names on his desk, of frog ceremony, of robot cartoons—such lifeless, joyless, unappealing things all of a sudden—then of his own watch. It was Ton-Ton's now, for sure, and he was surprised that he did not care. Of what use was a watch if the world was coming to an end, after all?

Kapayapaan Lobby

for Jean

Kapayapaan Lobby was simply a square in the center of a one-story rectangular building, built for student organizations. It had wooden tables and benches on each of its four corners, and double doors to its east and west that opened out to the rest of the university. A narrow hallway led from the lobby to the organization rooms in the north and south wings.

To Andy, the lobby was aptly named. He really did feel at peace here, sitting in his usual place almost beside the hallway that went on to the south. He didn't mind the general noise of students, shouting from doorway to doorway or down the length of the hall, crowding on the benches and tables and by the payphone, or lining up for the water fountain across the hallway from him. The ceaseless buzz soothed him, provided companionable white noise as he threaded his lonely way through the works of Marcel and Proust, Descartes and Kant.

More often than not, a group of Marketing and Business Management majors gathered around a table to his right, discussing and arguing about plans, accounts, and strategies. Some of them had already made his acquaintance, an expedient move because he proved a valuable resource person when ethics came into the picture, and when Philosophy Orals were scheduled. Across from them, a barkada of Political Science and History majors continually played pusoy dos, betting with loose change and cigarette sticks. A girl in a baseball cap, and with a cigarette tucked behind her ear, usually dealt out the cards. When she had to go to class, her boyfriend kissed her smack on the lips and replaced her as dealer. It amazed Andy how the whole gang could keep at it, game after game, replacing each other when the bell rang, or watching and coaching at the side while pretending to type up a paper on their communal manual typewriter.

Across the hallway, behind the water fountain and the occasional line of students, the glee club practiced their repertoire at full volume. Sometimes they practiced in groups of sopranos, altos, tenors, or bass. If one never left the lobby, it was still possible to tell what part of the schoolyear it was—church songs in July in anticipation of the Feast of St Ignatius,

Kapayapaan Lobby

Christmas carols during December to generate funds for the college's many outreach programs, and love songs in February for the school concerts and a number of Romeos who wanted to serenade their Juliets. In the final corner, assorted students sat for lunch or gossip or study or project, or to wait for their turn at Manang Doris' Xerox machine, one peso per page. No one stayed long in that final corner except Manang Doris herself, because her machine made the area too warm for comfort. One of the Business Management students had already suggested putting up an iced tea booth there, but his idea was immediately shot down by a long line of reasons that had to do with feasibility and being humane.

    Andy felt one with the world here, happy with the lobby's regularity, the way he was able to tell that the 1:30 bell had rung when a particular girl walked into the east door and drank from the water fountain, and then turned to walk into one of the rooms north of the lobby; or that it was 6:45 because Manang Doris began to close shop, locking her moneybox with a little silver-colored padlock, stacking all the long and short bond together in the wooden cabinet below the Xerox machine, and locking that up too. The moneybox, she would take home, the Xerox machine, she would unplug, roof with a wooden cover, lock with a key, and wheel to the northwest wall.

He also enjoyed the random surprise the lobby offered, few and far between so that he wasn't unpleasantly distracted —a student walking in looking like a stereotype nerd or jock, or a theater person suddenly booming his lines for the next school play, or, of course, Danielle the freshie, seeking him out for a particular problem in Mathematics (his other forte), or a brief hug and a long chat because her crush had spoken with her at length, or had said hi, or had talked to another girl instead of her. Danielle, whom he had met when he volunteered last summer to be part of the Registration Committee, counted as a surprise because she never came at any one given time, and would often disappear for days and days. She would have driven the fox and/or the Little Prince crazy.

One August afternoon, while the glee club yo-yoed up and down their scales and geared up for the September intercollegiate concert contest, Danielle paid another one of her surprise visits. He had been watching the water fountain girl bend to drink, studying the curve and blush of her left cheek, admiring the curl that was tucked neatly behind her left ear, and checking his watch to see if it was indeed 1:30 pm, when he felt Danielle's hand clutch at his right arm.

"Andrew," she said ever so sweetly, in lilting tones that challenged the mighty sopranos, "I've got to show you something." She wanted him to stand, to actually leave his spot even though it was not time for any of his classes, just to show him "something." He wasn't really that interested, he found, not as interested as staying in place and reading on about Levinas and "the face." But her face shone before him, her rosy lips pleaded, "Please Andrew, let's go," and her soft, cold, and tiny hands tugged at his arm. He found himself led out the eastern door, down a path to the university quadrangle, and made to look at a scene playing out under an acacia tree.

It was Danielle's crush, holding hands with another, whispering in her ear, rubbing noses with her, giving an exorbitant number of hugs, and all but necking. "The bastard," Andy cursed, for Danielle's sake.

"The cheat!" Danielle nodded, shaking a tiny fist at the gigantic acacia.

"The traitor," he added sympathetically.

"The heartbreaker!" and Danielle burst into tears so that he had to lead her to the nearest bench, making sure that they had their backs turned to the heartless romance unfolding. But Danielle kept looking over her shoulder and crying inconsolably. There had been hints, there had been words that were almost promises, Kent had no doubt led her on.

This time, it was Andy who looked behind him, but only to frown at those huge, frightening, weight-trained biceps, Kent Perez being the school's most-prized fencing champion. Besides, Andy reminded himself, he was a peace-loving humanitarian, more prone to acts of commiseration than to acts of violence. So, as tenderly as possible, he took Danielle into his arms. Danielle, taking one last look at Kent, and letting go one last sob, kissed Andy on the lips.

The next day, and the day after that, and the week after, until it was more than a month, Andy found himself making a beeline for the cafeteria where Danielle sat at a table with her girlfriends. True, he missed his spot in Kapayapaan Lobby from time to time, during an unusual moment of silence, or as he walked across the quadrangle after Logic or Liberation Theology class, or as he glimpsed the crowded Xerox machine of Aling Puring, 60 centavos a page. Then again, there was much to entertain him at the cafeteria, which he considered a bigger Kapayapaan Lobby.

There were, after all, similar double doors to the east and west, which opened to the rest of the university. To the north,

Kapayapaan Lobby

a counter displayed its variety of home-cooked viands, and hid, with the help of its staff and a low wall, a kitchen, where issued forth a cacophony of pots, pans, plates, and silverware. To the south, there stood a number of stalls, for fastfood, junkfood, an assortment of juices and flavored coffee, and of course, iced tea.

The rate of return and exchange here was more frequent, and, although spotting a familiar face was easier than he expected, the faces never stayed permanently at the same table, but moved all around the huge room. Andy had to admit to himself that life was indeed more exciting here, judging from just the number of interesting things that he could spot in a day. The plenitude of sameness which showed up at the door, stall, or table, for example, were more than he could count: girls all dressed in spaghetti straps or no straps at all, their heels two inches or higher; boys in knee-length shorts and Nikes of the latest model; ectomorphs behind thickest rims and heaviest lenses. The theater people often appeared here as well—in twos, in threes, in whole groups—clearing a space or joining tables for a stage, and booming their acts without the help of loudspeakers. And then, of course, there was Danielle every day, Danielle after every class, Danielle who was proud to show off to her friends a relatively good-looking and decent boy-next-door type who made irregular appearances in the Dean's List at the end of one semester or another.

Andy simply had to admit how fine life was, surrounded by young girls who all doted on him and needed him to help them with their Math, their Poetry, their Reflection Papers, and their crush-troubles. And if Kent ever sauntered in, at one or the other hour, and said hi, or lingered to talk a while, or walked right past with a girl herded by the crook of his arm, Andy just smiled magnanimously, because he knew that no matter what, and often sooner than later, Danielle would come to sit beside him and lean her smooth brow upon his solid shoulder.

And then, one day, in early January, after faltering in his Midterm Orals on Plato because he had failed to read up on some of the chapters, Andy, hands in his pockets, followed his feet back to the eastern door and to his regular spot in Kapayapaan Lobby.

Day after day, and the week after, until it was more than a month, Andy retraced his steps back to the quiet and dependable usual. It did not disturb him as much as he expected, the fact that Kent had finally come to his senses and become a regular at Danielle & co's table, without ever having a girl in the crook of his arm. It did not disturb him as much as he expected, the fact that Danielle had sat farther and farther away, an inch at a time, from his solid shoulder, and trilled her mighty soprano away from him instead of at him. Andy simply settled back into his quiet nook, which had thankfully and faithfully waited for him to return, and picked up where he left off with Plato and the more dependable Greeks.

Andy let himself be comforted by the constancy of the lobby, which was more than he could say about a certain Danielle. If from time to time, lyrics weeping of rejection and loss or brimming with the optimism and hope of love reached out to twang at his heart, Andy simply bore all stoically, until the moment passed, and he was able to appreciate once more the amazing, never-ending, enthusiastic game of pusoy dos before him, girl with baseball cap and cigarette rolling up her sleeves, or to eavesdrop upon the next ongoing debate on the feasible and the ethical. He read as he had never read before, to the humming of Manang Doris' Xerox Machine. He looked forward to the 1:30 appointment of the girl at the water fountain, and noticed that she now wore her hair short and manly, but with the curl still tucked behind the left ear. Even the curl was more constant than Danielle.

He felt safe and sound here, loved even, regarded by a pair of eyes that he could never quite find. Nevertheless, it fortified

Andy, made him feel more comfortably himself than Danielle's brow on his shoulder had ever done, made his soul sing as beautifully as the glee club on their best days. Grateful, he would look up from his books and seek those eyes, which, he was sure, knew him and loved him just as he was. He studied the girl with the baseball cap, yapping happily away as she tossed the cards about; he observed the girl at the fountain, silently drinking long draughts of water as she clutched a notebook to her chest; he even watched Manang Doris as she packed up her machine with the precision of the snappiest soldier. He peered into each and every female face of the glee club, their lips uniformly rounded, cheeks all hollowed out, foreheads furrowed in fierce concentration. He also, though he felt queasy at the thought, caught himself looking at two or three men of a feminine persuasion. But the owner of those eyes escaped him each time.

On Valentine's Day, as Andy turned a page of the *Dialogues*, several things happened. The girl with the baseball cap emptied her box of cigarettes on the floor and flung her cards at her boyfriend, screaming obscenities. Her boyfriend stretched out a hand to appease her, but she merely swatted at it. Stomping away, she noticed Andy watching and crossed her eyes at him. As she walked out, the girl who came to the fountain walked in, carrying a pile of library books. He craned his neck for a glimpse of their spines—ah, de Saint-Exupery, and oh, Camus!—then met her eyes for a second, and saw that her eyelashes curled the same darling way that the curl at the back of her ear did. As she bent over the fountain, a boy with a swing to his hips accosted her and whispered something in her ear that made her blush and choke. Both their heads turned towards Andy. The boy's eyes glinted so piercingly that Andy had to look away, sure that those were not the eyes he was looking for. Then Manang Doris' machine broke down, and Andy decided not to look.

When the maintenance man arrived with tools, the Glee Club was in the middle of a serenade for a couple who sat beside the broken Xerox machine. As the maintenance man waited respectfully for the end of "When You Say Nothing At All," Andy felt a familiar soft hand upon his arm, and a high shrill in his ear, "Oh Andrew, how I've missed you!"

Andy and Danielle hit upon a happy compromise—half the time she would stay with Andy in Kapayapaan Lobby, and half the time she would still spend with her girlfriends at the cafeteria, despite the fact that she had been replaced by her best friend in the crook of the arm of a particular Kent.

Andy didn't mind that from time to time, Danielle would sigh upon his solid shoulder, as if she were still heartbroken.

If anything, Andy was a forgiving person, and part of the paradigm that he had set for himself was to always view a person as intrinsically good, even Kent Perez. So day after day, until the month ended with Senior Final Exams and his graduation loomed near, Andy sat with a penitent Danielle against his shoulder, reading his books or solving her math problems, listening in on the girl with the baseball cap and pusoy dos, on arguments and feasibilities and strategies, on the Alma Mater song. Every day, he greeted Manang Doris as he took his usual place and waited for Danielle, and every evening, he waved her and her moneybox off as the clock ticked to seven.

What Andy did mind was the feeling that something was missing, that something had been driven away, that although he was showered with hugs and little kisses from Danielle, as well as winks from the Marketing and Business Management majors, something had changed irrevocably in the lobby's scheme of things. When he pored over his books, he felt increasingly lonely, enveloped by an emptiness that not even the Glee Club's fervent shouts could pierce. There were now many eyes upon him, now that this twittering, flittering bird had perched upon his shoulder and shared his space and complained petulantly about the cigarette smoke, but there was one pair that was missing, which his suddenly clouded mind could not identify. He simply had to accept that everything was in constant flux, that change was the only certainty, and that the intentional curl upon Danielle's brow, for some reason, made him want to weep.

The Grand Jeté

So you have always wanted to be a prima ballerina. Never mind that you tread on flat and strange-shaped feet, with ping-pong ball-sized bunions, so that when you point them high, they look like flying saucers, and when you point them low, they look like ostriches about to go underground. Never mind that the class takes away your Saturday morning cartoons and ends an hour after the time you are supposed to have lunch. Never mind that your stomach sours each time your teacher praises the girl next to you, then criticizes your posture, your plié, the curve of your arms, your fifth position.

Never mind that when you wait for Ate Leila in the advanced class, you see that they wear a different kind of shoe that squares at the toes and feels like cement. Never mind that after their class, you see that when they put their feet up on the bench to untie their laces, their legs jiggle involuntarily. Never mind that when you go on your first airplane trip, you see your ballet teacher take the whole trip with her legs in the air.

Never mind that when your class finally does turns, you can't understand what "spotting" means. Never mind that when they say it means keeping your eye on one portion of the wall, you simply end up cross-eyed. Never mind that when you attempt your turns, the room turns with you and you feel terribly sick, as sick as when you took your airplane ride, and thank goodness this time, you have no food in your stomach. Never mind that when you finally manage a turn, you land in an entirely different place from where you planned, and it is on somebody else's toe. Never mind that your best friend, whom you have bumped ten million times, makes comments on your bovine grace. Never mind that after five years, when you are about thirteen, everyone else moves on to the advanced class and you outgrow—and give up ever wearing—Ate Leila's hand-me-down toe shoes. And finally, never mind when your teacher suggests to your mother that you should take up swimming.

So you take up swimming in your fourteenth year. Your swimming instructor looks rather cute, so you are able to persuade your best friend to join you Mondays, Wednesdays, and Fridays. You both like the way his longish, curly hair sticks close to his head as if it were gelled back, and the way his heroic muscular arms hold on to you, never to let you drown. You are proud that when you finally master the arm movements and the kick of the breaststroke, your instructor says, just as your best friend emerges beside you, "Do you dance ballet?"

The Grand Jeté

    Your best friend imagines that each time your instructor rises from the pool, she can see a darker patch at the front of his yellow shorts. You giggle knowingly with her and pretend you can see it too, although you can't ever really describe how small or how large the patch is. Your heart flutters a bit each time he holds you just below the water as you practice your strokes and your kicks. You like that sometimes, you are sprayed with a little water when he shows you the right way to tilt your head and move your arms, or when he turns to your best friend to give her the same instructions. He always gives you the instructions first. Your heart breaks a little when your instructor turns to your mother one day and says your body seems too soft for swimming, and although you are graceful when you do your strokes, you are too slow, and therefore often sink. But you feel quite affirmed when he tells your mother that you should be taking ballet.

    You are a little bit annoyed that your best friend stays on with her swimming, and reports to you little things your former swimming instructor does that mean he has a crush on her—squeezing her on the shoulder, tucking a lock of her hair back into her swimming cap, and hugging her tight when she wins her first, very minor, competition. But you like it that your mother has enrolled you in another ballet class, with a different teacher, who praises you for the gracefulness of your neck, your arabesque when you raise your right leg backwards, your first position, and your smile. You make many more friends, although they all seem two or three years younger, and none of them ever comments on how your body seems to have become a little bit more beefy. The first time you ever see your teacher frown at you is when you finally do your turns. And, although you never bump into anyone this time, you still have to stop attending classes because you fall and need sixteen stitches under your chin.

When the thirty-something doctor with the boyish haircut holds you by the chin to check on your stitches, you consider being a doctor for thirty minutes before you realize you could just marry one, preferably one with a boyish haircut. In college, you realize ballet is still your calling when your PE teacher keeps scolding you for lifting a leg backwards each time you try to make the volleyball go over the net. You further decide that you have just received a message from heaven when a pre-Med guy who is your classmate in History says he saw you at the covered courts and thinks your habit of lifting your leg pretty cute. Because he has called you pretty, you decide that he is the guy you are destined to marry. Then one day, you must serve the volleyball and it once again goes under the net, but this time the ball hits your teacher smack where he lives and he asks slowly and politely and rather gaspingly if you would prefer to be in another PE class, so you say "Ballet." You then think God is taking matters into His own hands.

So you are back on track and pas de bourrée-ing and grand jeté-ing down the right path to your destiny. Never mind that your real course is Management. Never mind that the pre-Med boy pinches your cheeks each time he sees you, but has

The Grand Jeté

made another girl his girlfriend. Never mind that you have to lie to your ballet teacher about a medical condition, telling her that your ears have a defect which prevents you from making your turns while keeping equilibrium. Never mind that your teacher simply grimaces at you and makes you the prince instead of the princess at the end-of-semester recital. Never mind that, although your role is crucial, all you have to do is wear tights and a doublet, walk around in black ballet shoes, and lend your elbow to Cinderella. Never mind that the pre-Med boy insults you by saying that you should have been a boy, because you would have looked quite handsome. Never mind that even after three semesters of ballet for PE, you are still just the prince. Never mind that when your mother attends the last end-of-the-sem recital, she tells you that you should think about a fruit diet because the next role you are given might be king instead of prince. And finally, never mind that you one day discover you can no longer touch your toes.

Because by then the pre-Med boy has gone on to Medicine, and his girlfriend has broken up with him for not spending enough time with her. And because by then your best friend has married her swimming instructor and made you maid-of-honor, saying she wouldn't have met him without you, and he hugs you fondly at the reception. And because by then, your favorite course adviser, upon hearing your background in ballet, says she has a friend who owns a small ballet company which needs a manager.

So here you are, a manager of prima ballerinas. So never mind.

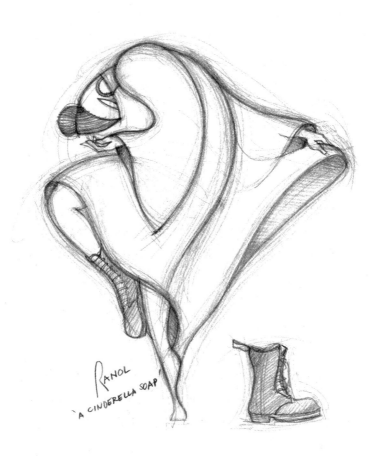

A Cinderella Soap

"I have nothing against you, I have nothing against you," the old crone cried, her crow's feet an inch from my face, ready to claw at me. She clutched at my shoulders and shook me until my neck felt rubbery and my head bobbed up and down.

As the world around me shuddered and swayed, I wondered, could this really be happening? Have I suddenly gotten myself into some soap opera? I waited as patiently as I could for the slap on my face.

But she only shook me further, as if she couldn't stop. "I have nothing against you, I have nothing against you!"

"Alright," I almost cried, "you've convinced me." But I remained stuck on the novelty of the soap. Why, was it not just three months ago, when his sister had called from her flat in New York, and I had chatted about my first semester in Boston before I realized what she was screaming in my ear—"Bitch! Bitch! Get away from my brother!"

Just when I felt the motion sickness kick in, his mother found new words to say. "I have nothing against you; just stay away from my son." She at last let go.

I could have defended myself: "I have stayed away. Haven't I avoided answering any of his letters? Wasn't he the one who came here today, looking for me, to say our final goodbyes?" Instead, I began to think I might be the defenseless underdog that the richest, kindest, handsomest young tycoon would someday marry. I tilted my head up, ready for the resounding slap. Only a whiff of wind hit my cheek as she turned and flounced away.

The son came too late for his cue. Had he been cowering in his mother's car all this time? Or had he thought that since we had already said goodbye, he need no longer defend me?

"What did she tell you?" he demanded.

I stared at him, stricken dumb by the thought that this guy had never slapped me before. Was he going to do so now? Oh please please please, then it would be so much easier to hate him.

He clenched and unclenched his hands, his eyes narrowing into stilleto knives. He was still waiting for an answer. I waited for my brain to expand once more, from the corner where it had been knocked over.

"She has nothing against me!" I cried triumphantly, and then, cheerfully, "Goodbye again."

A Cinderella Soap

His beautiful brown face, the perfect squarish chin, the piercing sad eyes, crumpled into a hurt expression. I must have said the wrong thing, I thought then, I must have stolen his line. It was I who had done the slapping. And off he went to his mommy.

Our common friend, and my neighbor, Rexy, came out of hiding from behind the stairs. "You're too nice, too goody-goody," he said sadly, like he had wanted to hear screaming and witness women tearing at each other's hair. He guided me to the steps as if I were a casualty of war, and it did seem like some of my limbs and internal organs were missing. He let me put my head down on his knee and weep.

The machinery up north stirred sluggishly into order. I found myself counting—one, never fall in love with a student, even if he is a former student, and especially if he is failing in all his subjects; two, age may not matter, so long as you look five years younger, but perhaps educational attainment does; three, actually, just never fall in love again; four, maybe it's better to be gay, or five, what if I started kissing Rexy; six, I want a boy's lips … no, not just lips, I want the whole boy!

I began to wail, but cut myself off when I noticed that Rexy, who had been stroking my hair, had it falling the wrong way, over his knee and sweeping his shoes. What did he want a free shoeshine for? I thought angrily, then realized something else. My bare nape was wet. The fool had been crying over me like some woman war victim over her dead. Which was probably what I was going to look like once I stood up with my face red, my eyes swollen, and my hair streaming down my front instead of my back.

"Rexy, dear," I said, delighted that my voice came out cracked and sultry.

"What?" he sobbed.

"Our beauty."

We looked into each other's red-rimmed eyes and grinned. Beauty was definitely much more important than crying over something that had ended some months back anyway. We wiped our tears and fixed up. While Rexy tucked his longish hair behind his ears, I stood up and dusted my jeans, readying myself to face what was to be the last few days of my Christmas vacation.

As Rexy kissed me goodbye at the departure gate of the Ninoy Aquino International Airport, I once again burst into tears at the thought that because I was old, I could no longer get what I wanted for Christmas. I had needed a fairy godmother so badly, but all I got was a fairy who would cease to be my friend once school began in January. Now Rexy would have my ex-prince all to himself, see him everyday, and perhaps even gossip with him about me.

A Cinderella Soap

"Hel-lo ... your beauty ..." Rexy warned, trying to smooth my hair down, and this time, the right way. "I know you'll miss ME," he added, winking, then kissing me again, this time on my forehead.

I turned my back silently on the Judas, and caught my father's look of disapproval. I never quite knew what he thought of my friendship with Rexy, five years my junior, and my former student, and worse, what to him was a screaming homo. He kissed me stiffly, then pushed me gently towards the softness of my mother. There was no plugging my leaking faucet, as I turned to kiss and drench her with tears. They would think it was homesickness, but if they found out ... no, not *if*, but *when* they found out, because the thought of Rexy, on the way home with them in the traffic of EDSA, made me sure that I was going to be betrayed that very day. I pushed past a three-generation clan saying their farewells to a balikbayan family and screeched to a halt at the end of a long line that led into the entrance of the airport.

Nothing could have made me look back. Was Rexy even then whispering everything to my mother? I kept my eyes staring straight ahead, thrust my passport into some hands, snatched it back, and gasped in relief as I burst through the door. They couldn't drag me out now, could they? Each step— of heaving up my luggage for X-ray and for check-in, of paying travel tax and going through the portals of immigration—

took me further away from the chance that my parents would run in to get me and flog me on the streets as the one who had brought shame down upon their venerable heads.

A couple of hours later, finally safe on the plane some thousand feet high in the clouds, I felt what was left of my sorry heart slow down. It was the perfect time to have a seizure and die, I thought, without having yet been scolded for my indiscretions, my improper behavior. But that would have happened only if fairy godmothers did exist. I pressed my nose to the window, turning my back on the people beside me with their socked feet out of rubber shoes. I knew I was lucky enough to have left my stink behind, at least for a while. And if I were luckier still, by the time I got home, the stink would have dissipated.

But what had become of me? I had hours and hours ahead to survey the damage, and to check if I had become the embittered spinster I feared becoming. And worse, if my actions these past couple of years had only proven me a loose and immoral woman. What had happened to the girl whose father and mother had taught to always be truthful, to never keep secrets from her parents, to never backbite or think ill of her friends? How could she have gotten herself involved in an underground relationship, and now think cynically of the one friend who was there when she got her heart broken?

A Cinderella Soap

"My God," I blurted, startling my neighbors out of their snores. "I've turned into a hag!"

The one nearest me, shifting his hefty weight and opening one lazy eye to look, said, "No you haven't."

"Thanks," I could have said. "Hey, thanks," I could have flirted. But my throat caught, and my mind steered away from the tousled, close-cropped brown hair, and the glinting blue eye, and instead focused on the carpet fuzz that had collected on his not-so-white socks, and the breath of garlic and peanuts. By the time we landed at Narita Airport for the first stopover, I felt properly nauseated, and let out all into the little bag for motion sickness.

∽ ∾

And so on I flew towards the East Coast and the winter of my discontent. I intended to suffocate with Shakespeare, blind myself in Milton, and then feed my angst with Eliot and Pound. These dead men were going to make me brilliant, as well as ensure my virginity for a long time yet, in a class of blonde, brown, and red-headed women, two black turtleneck-wearing gays, and the Asian quota of Ya Hui and me.

Inside the freezer that was Boston, my first task after jet lag was to go to the library and borrow as many of the required books as I could carry in my trusty Eastpak. On my way back to the dorms, I found to my dismay that I had forgotten to factor in the snow, which had frozen and dirtied and hardened and grayed through the long holidays. It had also become more slippery. At the curb, beside which stilled and steaming vehicles waited for the traffic light to turn green, the weight on my back could no longer resist gravity. My duck shoes skidded and flew up in the air, with the rest of me in tow.

The Hyundai nearest me erupted in unrestrained laughter, and from the ground I glimpsed four hideous Caucasian mouths grinning down at me. "Hey, little girl, are you alright?" the one with the creamy moustache called from the death seat. I waited for the lights to turn green before picking myself up, not wanting to show them any more Monkey tricks, all the while Jack Frost nipped at my nose and my heart chilled.

Men are beasts, I thought. Would that be an acceptable thesis statement? Were there animal references to the male characters in any of my classes? Men are beasts, and worldly, while women, while the marginalized ... but classes hadn't even begun, so what did I know? As I crossed the street to the dorms, I entertained myself with the thought of my new look before the winter was over—a boy's cut, white woolen sweaters and blue jeans, and the industrial Doc Martens with the black laces. Nobody would ever mistake me for a little girl then.

As I let myself into my dormitory, I looked through the glass window into the security room, and glimpsed a fresh new face looking back at me. His brown eyes smiled with the rest of him, and my heart skidded in imitation of my back flip a few minutes before, sending my thesis statement into the trash bin. "Kate, Kate, Kate, Kate, Kate," I knocked on the door next to my room.

"What?" she said, opening wide. I could see her at one glance in her robe, hair bleach on her arms and above her upper lip, towel wrapped around her head like a turban.

I remembered the moustache first. "I fell," I said. She let me in, and, as I narrated what those mean Americans had done, tucked me under the warm covers of her quilt, handmade by the Amish who lived a few hours away from her family home in Pennsylvania.

"Don't worry about them," she said, bowing, letting her curly chesnut hair tumble out of the towel, and exposing her nape. That immediately made me think of Rexy, but I wasn't about to tell her the childish things I had done a continent and an ocean away.

"Let's go shopping this weekend. I'd like to buy new shoes."

Kate raised her fine-lined eyebrows, and looked pointedly at the foot of her bed, where I had taken off the cumbersome winter galoshes. "You just bought those last term when it began to snow."

"I know, but they pinch my toes and make them numb with the cold."

"Oh, poor baby," Kate said mockingly, but she smiled, so I knew we had a shopping date that weekend. "Is that what was so urgent?"

"Yeah," I said, twanging happily at the thought of Doc Martens. I hid under the quilt so that Kate could dress and I could thaw, and so that she couldn't see that I was about to tell her something more. No, there wasn't anything more. I wasn't about to have a crush on a security guard.

∽ ∾

By Saturday evening, all I had to show for our shopping cruise was a stomach bulging from two bowls of clam chowder and a knitted white sweater with a baby pink collar, chosen for me by Kate because I couldn't choose for myself. For some reason, I was suddenly frightened of offending Kate in her woolen skirt and angora sweater, and steered clear of all masculine-looking shoe stores, although I allowed for one trip to the bargain racks of Filene's, before I shook my head and decided to bear with the shoes on my feet. I felt terribly ugly, but then, who was I to look pretty for anyway?

In the middle of the night, after a trip to the communal bathroom, a pile of fashion magazines on top of the trash bin caught my eye. I felt compelled to study them more closely, right there in the hallway; and then, as page after page of sophisticated-looking women paraded before my eyes, I began to learn a little bit more about glamour, and how hopeless it was for me. I had to grow taller, and to starve myself first, both impossible things to do considering my genes and my love for everything sweet. I felt so troubled by this that I had to close my eyes for a while and lean my elbows upon the flat surface of the trash bin.

While in that absurd pose, the door swung open and the fresh-faced security guard strode in, keys jingling, walkie-talkie crackling. "Hello," he called, not ten feet away from where I stood, so that I could see the shiny clean-cut hair, the browns of his eyes, the ruddiness of his cheeks, the silver pinky ring as he waved. "Hi," I could have said casually, "how's it going?" but I had turned tail before I could compose myself, scattering a pile of magazines in my wake, leaving him in his tracks with no glass slipper on hand.

I slammed my door shut and dove for my bed, screaming into my pillow. Stupid, stupid, ugly girl! And as I cried myself to sleep, I could see what he must have seen—a bag lady in her granny nightgown.

By mid-February, I had mastered the art of looking straight ahead as I let myself into the dorm. My first paper in Modern Poetry generated so much class discussion that at least, for one day, I drifted into the dorm, forgetting completely the glass-windowed security room beside it. Kate caught up with me at the foot of the stairs. "What's the matter with you?" she asked. "You walked right past security."

For a split second, I thought that Kate had found me out. And then of course, I came to my senses, remembering that everyone had been asleep when I took that midnight stroll to the bathroom and back, and bumped into the pinky ring prince.

"So?" I asked, attempting nonchalance. "We walk right past security each day." I grinned at my own wit.

"Yeah," she said, in a tone much like Rexy when he was being sarcastic. "Except that this security guard was tapping on the glass and waving this envelope in the air." Kate proceeded to demonstrate, then handed me a sealed airmail envelope. I checked the return address and laughed. Speaking of the devil. Then I saw Kate's raised eyebrows and the curious searching look. "You didn't even notice him," she said, exasperated. "You didn't even notice that he was cute."

"Who?"

She stomped her foot, and a clod of snow scattered. "The security guard."

"Oh, is he?"

"Yes," she hissed, and I recognized the urgency of her lust, very much like the pounding I did at her door the very first day I saw him.

A Cinderella Soap

"Rats," I said, teasing her and meaning it at the same time, but also, I was distracted by the letter in my hand. At the door of my room, before Kate could invite herself in, I said, "Oops, gotta get my reading done for tomorrow. See you at breakfast, Kate."

Unable to wait any longer, my winter coat and shoes making a puddle on the floor, I tore the envelope and read.

Dear Beautyfic Beauty, Rexy wrote. *Thanks for your letter.* But I was too impatient to read it from beginning to end. My father and mother had not mentioned anything in all my phone calls to them, but I wanted Rexy to confirm that they had found out nothing, so that I knew they weren't just worried about the extra dollars a scolding over long distance would cost. I scanned the page, and something else jumped out at me:

Your ex was angry to hear about your wanting your letters back. I couldn't even explain about the nightmares you are having because of them, kasi he suddenly punched the hood of his car, nagtarush! Oh, and one time, we saw each other at Hard Rock. He brought a date named Nadia. But don't worry, mas gwapa ka, dear. And she kept asking naman about you – not knowing anything but that you're an ex. Me naman, siyempre, super build up sa iyo. Too bad for your ex, he must have realized what he lost. So chugi si Nadia – he stood up and danced with some other girl. Unfortunately, he chose one that was drunk, and she broke her ankle on the dance floor!

I whooped. I couldn't resist it. I raised two champion's fists in the air, jumped, hugged myself, and blew a flying kiss for Rexy, thinking, That's my fairy godmother!

∽ ∾

I never did get to tell my parents about the day I defiled our home with the drama at the foot of our stairs—a drama that, with time and distance, now seemed laughable. I did tell my mother the truth that I had a crush on our security guard, "who is a working student, actually," I added, so that she wouldn't worry. And then I convinced her to let me use her Citibank extension card, kept for emergencies, so that I could buy me a pair of shoes in March. It would, I said, serve as her and my father's birthday gift.

That very Saturday, on a basement store along Newbury St, I enjoyed the look of shock on Kate's face as I pointed at the pair of shoes I wanted, its black leather as shiny as the gloss on its brown rubber soles. "Those," I said to her. "Size six," I told the blonde salesman.

"You want Doc Martens?" she asked. "Are you sure?"

"Yes," I practically hummed, "they're rounded, see, and won't pinch my toes."

Kate shook me by the shoulders. "Are you sure? Are you well?"

"Oh, cut the drama, Kate."

A Cinderella Soap

Kate grinned. "Why, I didn't know there was a tough girl in you."

"Yeah," I said, " I sure had you fooled." With fellow feeling for Kate, I decided I wouldn't cut my hair as short as a boy's just yet. She could only take so many shocks in one day. Besides, I thought, I might still have a use for long hair, to flick at that security guard in case he ever looked my way or said hello again.

I was starring in a shampoo commercial, playing out in my mind, when the blonde salesman came back, with the shoes looking crisp in their brown, square-shaped box. He knelt and slid the shoes neatly onto my feet, the right, and then the left. I took my time tying the laces, then stomped in them awhile before I glanced at the mirror. And when I looked at my feet there, shod in the sturdy-looking Doc Martens, I gave the salesman and Kate the thumbs up sign.

"These shoes fit perfectly," I said.

The Line

"Hello Mahal," he says, and the connection is choppy, cutting up the usual rounded and satisfying sound of his tenor. No matter, she feels hugged by his new term of endearment anyway (last week she had been called "Princess"). Her heart squelches, and heaves up as if to tug for more of his words. She hates it when it does that, and hates to be reminded of sappy telephone commercials. "And how are things there?"

"Great," she replies. At the same time, she grasps for things at the edges of her mind—things she had made mental notes of, worthy anecdotes, decisions that they both have to make; things that may be important to mention before he has to hang up. "How are you?" she asks in return, to give herself time to gather her thoughts.

"Great," he says. "Girlie—"

"Joaquin—"

They both pause, waiting politely for the other to speak first. She can say "Oh, nothing," or blurt out one thing or another. She decides on, "So, is it getting cold there?"

"Oh, you can't be-lieeeve this weather," he answers, almost sounding too emphatic to her ears. But he says it in just the same way that he speaks about things that excite or amuse or annoy him—"Can you be-lieeeve that pass? The Rums better shape up;" "Can you be-lieeve that driver? She's a woman, no doubt;" "Can you be-lieeve our president? Our country will never recover again."

He has had a sampling of all the seasons in New York, and is moving on to his second year there. "I wish you were here," he says, now softly, and she strains her ears for any note of insincerity, any sign of the opposite.

She knows she is being paranoid; she has often admitted this to herself and to anyone whom she thinks must be warned. She has also known that it is this trait that might someday make her a stereotypical nagging wife, that might ruin any sort of normal relationship with a husband, as it had ruined countless of past relationships already. So, she is still often surprised to find herself having finally crossed over, having joined her line of friends who have already tied the knot.

Her friends are still just as surprised by her move—why had she agreed to marry Joaquin, when she knew that he was planning to go to America to work? How would they be able

The Line

to endure the distance? How did she think herself into believing that she could?

"So have you decided? Are you coming home this Christmas?"

She can't erase the longing in her voice, and she fears that he might be put off by it.

"I'm not sure," he says. "If I work extra hours at customer service during the holidays, then we might have even more savings." It is always "we" with them when it comes to money. And though he has never mentioned the possibility of her joining him, he has assured her several times that when he has earned enough, then he can come home, and she can move out of the house she boards in, and they can begin to think about having a family. But how much is enough? Why has she never thought—or rather, dared—ask him this?

"It's just October," he reminds her, and he is right, of course. But then, it is also almost November, and she hates to be kept in suspense. "So," and he sounds more at ease now, ready to have a rolling conversation with her, "what are you wearing?"

She laughs, a little bit hysterically, she thinks, and then she remembers the warmth of his presence, as he used to stand behind or beside her, always with an arm around her neck. Has it already been a year since the last time? She can still think about his hand on her breast and shudder with delight. Still, there had been no child to bring him back at once—she knew she had wished for something of the kind, but would never admit it to anyone. She prides herself on being capable and independent, a "low maintenance" sort of gal. She wonders if that is what men like after all, and how she might be a little bit more "high maintenance" and still likable.

"No, seriously," he persists.

"Oh don't start," she chides, and then laughs much more naturally, as she tries to find a better position for her phone, where there is less static. She finds herself indulging him anyway. "Nothing. I'm in my room and trying to save on laundry soap." He laughs and says something about how he has come up with a system of doing the laundry.

Her friend, Leny, seems to be just such a one—an independent, modern woman with a flourishing career in investment banking; yet ever-demanding when it comes to her husband. "He has to be more sensitive to my needs," she complains, each time Girlie meets with her in the Starbucks nearest Leny's office, all the while waving right under Girlie's nose the most recent letter her husband has penned. Girlie often feels hurt by that; she never has any letters with which to show off her own husband's love for her. The phone bills aren't exactly a romantic enough equivalent, and each time she gets them, she suffers an anxiety attack and needs to work out the next month's budget yet again, to calm herself. In the back pages of

The Line

her planner, there are columns for her expenditures, and each month she writes down her expenses for Globe Handyphone as well as her share in the boarding house's PLDT bill.

Now Joaquin teases her about really just asking this girl in his office to wash his underwear with hers. She flinches, but does not let herself react. She is also trying to decide whether to tell Joaquin that Leny's husband has, once again, flown off for a month on a business trip, this time to Spain; and that, once again, Leny could not join him, because of the demands of her own work. But Girlie worries he might think that somehow she is comparing him to Leny's husband, or their married life to Leny's, which might be dangerous.

"Hello? Hello!" Joaquin's voice comes in fragments, like a dancer under a strobe light. And then they are cut off.

The screen on her mobile phone reveals that her battery must be charged soon. She attaches her phone to its charger, which she rarely keeps unplugged now, and lies down on her bed to wait. Joaquin has instructed her that he should always be the one to call her, unless during emergencies, because it is cheaper that way. She wonders if her attacks of paranoia might count as emergencies, whenever she feels like calling him to catch him in the act. In the act of what? She would rather not pursue this line of thinking.

Just two days ago, Leny had called to ask Girlie to meet her in Starbucks because she had "thrilling kwento." Girlie had a deadline to meet for the *Sunday Lifestyle* magazine, but didn't know how to say no.

"I've got a man," Leny says immediately, in the act of sitting down and putting her handbag and chic leather briefcase on the empty chair beside her. She makes no apology for being late for thirty minutes, and doesn't notice that Girlie has already finished her mocha frapuccino with time to spare for regretting the calories. "A client of mine. Married. With children. We meet for lunch sometimes."

And then she looks worriedly into Girlie's eyes. "Are you shocked? It's harmless fun, really, we flirt, he calls me 'baby,' I call him 'hunkie'." Leny warms up. "He texts me some green jokes. And, we've held hands a couple of times." She says it breathlessly, then meets Girlie's eyes again. "He is my textmate." She whispers it, looking to her left and to her right, as if she has said something illicit, like "He is my lover." But she has distinctly said "textmate." Has she meant it to be some kind of code? There is no telltale winking.

Girlie remembers her father—every time she goes to visit her childhood home in Cebu—shaking his head at what he pronounces "American values," while she watches *Ally McBeal* or *Sex in the City* with him. He would sniff and snort and chuckle softly, each time a woman and a man hopped into bed, each time they exchanged partners, or fought and argued and discussed their tangled-up relationships. She feels him

The Line

justified, though, in turning up his nose at them. After all, he has remained faithful to her mother for thirty-five years now. They are still in love, or he has no cause to complain, for her mother still does everything for him, and her mother still clearly worships the ground he walks on. She wonders if he would consider Leny's "thrilling kwento" as a sign of "American values."

Girlie finds herself un-thrilled, and slightly disturbed. Leny seems to see this, and says, "I've told Edwin," and she giggles. "He is jealous, of course, and phoned long distance to have some shop send me roses." If Edwin, her husband, knows, then it should be okay, is what she seems to imply. Later, she exclaims, rather regretfully, "Oh, I married too early!" Girlie wonders if this is a legitimate excuse for unfaithfulness, supposing, of course, that Leny's activities could be considered unfaithful. Could having married too late also be an excuse for other particular situations? Other situations like what? She doesn't know.

Girlie is curious to know what Joaquin might think, but when her phone finally blinks and tinkles the tune that now slightly irritates her, she has decided not to say anything. She knows she will stammer, because she is unsure, and Joaquin might misjudge Leny. If he does, then Girlie will think of herself as having betrayed her best friend.

"Hey," Joaquin says. "Did you put the phone down? Are you angry?"

It takes Girlie some time to recall the thread of their conversation.

"Are you jealous?" Joaquin needles, and she feels a wave of annoyance run through her.

"You just take so much pleasure in making me jealous," she accuses, and they both know that this is true, and that it hurts her.

"Oh sorry, sorry," Joaquin says, using his baby voice, then quickly changes the subject. "The company is picking up again, my boss is thinking of making some of us permanent." Joaquin works for a software company, and Girlie is sure, without being told, that he impresses his colleagues with his impeccable work ethic. She can also imagine their awe, how he can appear so cheerful, how he can banter with anyone and get away with it, how he can seem to be doing nothing, and yet be the first to get everything done. She is proud of this, this is what made Joaquin alluring to her, the first time she had met him in college. He was never seen studying, would be with her until late at night at her boarding house, and then he would top their exams in Math and History and Science the next day.

"I'm sure Mr Thorne will choose you."

The Line

He sighs. "Let's hope so, Girlie, then I can go home soon and spend my life with you."

She shivers, and finds herself confused. On one level she again ponders why she always seems surer of him than he is about himself. On another, she thinks about why she feels guilty for finding fault with the sweetest things that Joaquin declares. Doesn't he see it too, his being so smart? How can he go home the moment he is promoted? When will he ever come home, or at least, visit? Why doesn't she just ask him this? She knows the answer—she fears putting him off, and since he is far away, he might resort to anything, anything at all. Like what? Again, she doesn't want to pursue this line of questioning. Everyone thinks that she has married a very stable man. She does think so too. Most of the time.

"Hey, you like that don't you?" he teases. "You like the thought of spending our lives together?"

She finds her opening. "When do you think, Joaquin?" Again there is longing in her voice, and she is ashamed of it, because people have judged her to be sweet based on that tone, and she knows that this uncontrollable tone doesn't reveal the real her at all. Not her whole self, at any rate, because there is also that part of her that is sharp and suspicious, and now, rather weary.

"Mr Thorne wants me to go to Chicago next weekend, for a seminar." She finds her opening closed. But she listens, interested, imagining Joaquin in a suit and tie, studying the curve of his shoulders and the glint of his shoes, enjoying the picture she has called to mind. She loves that she can still see his face, although no longer where his moles are. The picture wavers when she tries to focus on his lips.

Her stable man is still rather unlike the stable husband of Joanna, her editor and friend. Girlie has glimpsed him because he is the owner of the magazine, and also a couple of publishing houses, and he strikes Girlie as too serious, too remote, and too still, and therefore the total opposite of bubbly and hilarious Joanna. She can't see how they can get along, has trouble imagining how it must be like when they're both home. If she can, then Girlie thinks she might be able to explain how Joanna can be very friendly with other men, but never in any scandalous sort of way. Girlie is very jealous of Joanna, who seems to have hit upon a wonderful balance. Even when her husband is on a trip somewhere, even when he disappears for a couple of months to visit his mother in Australia, Joanna always seems content to be by herself, or with friends, or surrounded by her many men, who like to confide in her, and who, like her, are happily married.

Joanna likes to confide in Girlie, especially about a particular male friend of hers. "Ben is my soulmate, supersure." Her soulmate is never her husband, but Ben. They like to inquire into the details of things, as her husband never does,

The Line

they like to compare notes about their children, and they laugh about the fact that they have named their children similar names—Lorelie and Lorenzo, Michelle and Michael. "It's really amazing ... when I dream of him, he calls the next day." Girlie has witnessed this for herself, for even as Joanna spoke of her dream over lunch one day, Ben rang up on her mobile. Girlie heard Joanna speak in subdued and even, measured tones, sounding so different from the Joanna she knew.

Girlie has lost the thread of what Joaquin is saying. She can't recall any of the details of the seminar, what it is all about; she doesn't know if Joaquin is going to Chicago or not. She plays safe, saying, "If you're being sent to a seminar, that means Mr Thorne is investing in you."

"Yes, yes," Joaquin replies, and he sounds impatient. Now he wants to know about her work, and she speaks half-heartedly, about an interview with a playwright, and her feature on Bohol. She has just spent last weekend in Bohol, but what can she tell him about the Chocolate Hills and her boatrides along the coast—there are no interesting events connected to the sights, no one beside her she could have shared them with. She knows that he isn't really listening either, that he must be preoccupied with something. She hears him typing on computer keys.

Girlie herself has a textmate, whom she also sometimes considers—or wishes to be—her soulmate. He is Joaquin's best friend, who works as a sportswriter in the same magazine. She likes it when he drops by and sits on her desk at work, and when he offers her his coffee from the same mug. She adores him, his boyish energy, indulges his Pan-like praise of himself, self-affirming and self-deprecating at the same time. She is thrilled by his certainty and judgment regarding everything under the sun. When he talks about his indiscretions with other women, most of whom are married, when he speaks of trying out particular drugs, or his increasing alcohol consumption, she feels distant, safe, protected, because she is married to somebody else who is much more responsible. But she likes the idea that Fernan seeks her out, that he finds it easy to confide in her. She feels proud that she has "got a man" too.

"Fernan got to interview Shaq when he came for a visit."

"Really?" Now Joaquin is more interested, and asks questions that she can sometimes answer, and sometimes cannot—what Shaq said, was he going to be traded, where he went, did he enjoy it in the Philippines. She begins to feel like a basketball player herself—with a fifty-fifty ratio at the freethrow line. Girlie is more interested in why she always has to find a way to include Fernan in their phone conversations. Is this her way of defining her relationship with Fernan, of legitimizing it? Is it illegal in the first place?

The Line

Technically speaking, no. But is she, as she thinks sometimes that Leny or Joanna might be, rationalizing something that cannot be rationalized? Are they completely truthful with themselves, and is it possible to be, and is that the best way to be anyway?

She often wants to ask her father why he describes the TV scenes of love and flirtation, sex and indiscretion, as showing "American values." True, the actors are American, but what about the local ads in newspapers and on television, showing a man surrounded by women, a woman surrounded by men, how exciting and glamorous to live in the moment, to act on immediate impulses. Girlie feels particularly intrigued by the portrayal of women—the more playful or flirtatious or sensual or modern the women, the more beautiful their dresses, the more graceful the curves of their necks, and the more shiny their hair. On some days when Fernan has paid particular attention to her, when he has given her a hug or a pinch on the cheek, when his rough hand brushes against her fingers as he shows her an article or hands her his mug, Girlie looks at herself in the mirror of the ladies' room and checks to see if she has not begun to look more like those women.

To herself, she only looks confused, and thoughtful. She begins to hear herself waxing like an obsessed romantic, that love nowadays seems to have become strange and unfamiliar.

There are too many distractions, too many ideals depending on whether on the physical or emotional or moral plane, too many categories and subcategories: just a friend, a special someone, housemate, textmate, soulmate. Where is pure and simple love—the one, true love that everyone expects and demands—among these? Perhaps, after all, there is no such love. No such thing as love? But that would be going too far.

She knows she doesn't always have to define things, even when she has the compulsion to. She doesn't even know how she feels about Fernan, which is probably why she feels drawn to him. She also, now that she thinks of it, sees in Fernan something terribly attractive, a godlike aura or quality that, if she accidentally touches—as Sleeping Beauty does the spindle—might make her lose herself. She sometimes catches herself wondering what it might be like to be kissed by him—would she find in his lips a draught of forgetfulness, or the spring of eternal youth? She dismisses such thoughts quickly, worried that they might already count as marital infidelity.

The computer keys have stopped clacking. Joaquin has asked her a question she has not heard. She has been too busy—the whole time, really—listening for sounds other than his voice, but there is only the silence, the pause as he waits for her answer. She hears the intake of his breath, as he listens, perhaps also wondering whom she might be with, what she might really be doing. Is there such a thing as male intuition?

The Line

"What?" she finally asks.

"Nothing," he says, "I have to go now."

They both fill up the line with their silences, and the line grows into a wall so thick that it spans their distance across the ocean. She stands on one side, and he on the other, and she wonders if he feels as lonely as she does, here on the shore where he has left her, as he braves a new world by himself. She sees herself waving on the shore, just as she says into the receiver, "Goodbye." Her heart once again squelches, for what does she really mean, exactly, when she says "Goodbye?"

The Patient

After evening Mass, Araceli found the other hospital bed empty and lay herself down upon it. She shut her eyes and breathed in the smell of medicine and clean sheets.

"Another patient is on the way, you know," Trining said from her seat across the room, the warning tone in her voice unmistakable. It meant: *Get up, don't fall asleep.*

Araceli smiled. She took a deep breath and felt herself sink deeper towards blessed sleep. A minute more, she told herself, that's all I need.

"Araceli!"

The fluorescent above burned orange through her eyelids. If only she had given me another minute, Araceli thought, and quickly sat up. The bed creaked in unison with her bones. The blood swam warmly full in her head and her sight blurred. She laughed.

"You be quiet, Celi, or you'll wake up Manang."

Gradually her eyes focused on the hospital bed across from hers, where huddled the unmoving figure of their eldest sister, Fortuna. At the foot of the bed was a moveable table for the patient's meals, which they used as a worktable, since Fortuna didn't mind eating with the tray on her bed. Trining sat on the sofa behind the table, bending over the rosary forming bead by bead in her hand.

Araceli watched her sister's other bony hand thread and knot the purple beads in smooth, uniform movements. Those gnarled, brownish hands had been soft and fair once, so many years ago. The pair had been a source of so much pride, making a fifteen year-old Trining pass on the dishwashing to her younger, eager-to-please sister Araceli. It had been ten years after the war, and there had no longer been any household help. Then too, Fortuna was still unmarried at twenty, and had become their parents' main concern. How could they ever have noticed the unequal distribution of chores?

Not that I really minded, Araceli thought, remembering those sleepy summer afternoons just after lunch. The wooden, two-story house that had replaced their hacienda, would settle solidly into the afternoon siesta. Araceli would take her time lathering each plate, alone with her fourteen year-old dreams of marriage and kitchens and babies. Every other day, she had planned, she would make butter cake for her family in

The Patient

the way her mother had taught her, with just the right amount of lemon. Her husband—handsome and strong, of course—would be able to buy her as much butter and flour as she wanted.

"Hoy, Celi, straighten out that bed already and put all our things on our side of the table."

Carefully, reminding herself of her bad back, Araceli got to her feet. After stretching the thin, white sheet flat out on the bed and re-tucking its edges between mattress and metal, Araceli turned to the bags scattered haphazardly on the long narrow table between the two beds. She put the paper bag still filled with puto in the Jollibee plastic bag with the three remaining ponkan oranges. The plastic forks and spoons from Tapa King, already washed after their meal yesterday, she placed in the other Jollibee bag among their own stainless steel utensils, plastic plates, and cups. The plate of one and a half cups of rice, covered with saran wrap, she set beside the two plastic bags. The sports bag, borrowed from Trining's son Noel, she stuck under the bed. She cleared some space at Fortuna's feet, beside their bag of threads, needles, beads, and the book that Araceli had dropped for the Mass at the hospital chapel. There, she eased herself into a sitting position.

"Let me see the leaves you've made," Trining said, without looking up.

She took her time with the bead of the Fifth Mystery, before she turned to the green-hued leaves Araceli had crocheted earlier and had now lined up on the worktable. She picked one that was olive green and frowned before putting it down. She poked the others with a wrinkled finger and said, "You do them too tight, Celi. Look how they don't lie flat on the table." The leaves, in fact, curled like Trining's hand, but Araceli liked them that way. It made them look more lifelike, somehow. "These won't do. It will make the runner bunch up once you sew them together."

"I'll make more tomorrow," Araceli said. She picked up *Little Women*, the book she was reading; re-reading, actually, and for the hundredth time. It had been her favorite when she was young. Now that she had retired and resettled in Pampanga, she thought she would enjoy it again, and had looked for it among the dusty hardbound books that lined the one and only bookcase behind her dining table.

She now lived again with her sisters in the same wooden, two-story house that her parents had left specifically to her. There had been those two landed brothers to marry off Fortuna and Trining to, but no third one. Therefore she had been promised the house. Araceli had kept re-reading that particular scene in *Little Women* when Mrs March told her daughters, Meg and Jo, that it was better to remain unmarried than to

The Patient

find a husband but live unhappily. Araceli's own mother had tried to comfort her on her nineteenth birthday. "Do not worry, hija, you are still young." She had wondered how her parents had found Fortuna old at twenty, when they could keep finding her young all through her twenties, not letting her go to Manila for college.

"Why do you need to go to college?" her father had asked, time and time again, with his arm around her. "Why not stay here with your Papa and Mama?"

How she had longed for independence then, to be like Jo March, who had gone off on her own to New York. Jo March had seen so many new things, had met all sorts of people, including, of course, her future husband.

"Celi," Trining broke through her thoughts, "you better hurry with those leaves if you want to finish by Martha's birthday." Martha was Noel's wife, the perfect daughter-in-law whom Trining loved and Araceli pitied.

Just as Araceli dropped the book and reached for her crochet needle, the door opened. Both Araceli and Trining paused, and Fortuna raised her head. The new patient, a pale and skinny girl of around twenty, greeted them with a wan smile as she was wheeled in. The attendant helped her up the bed and under the thin bedsheet, and hung up her IV bottle. He bade them all goodnight before he left with the wheelchair.

The girl conversed in low tones with her companion, a boy of the same age. He showed her where he was putting her things—her shoulder bag and cellphone on the table beside her, the green knapsack at her feet.

"I'll call you when I get home," he said, kissing her on the forehead and smoothing from her face her straight, shoulder-length hair. "Goodnight, sweetheart." At the door he turned to the three sisters and caught Araceli's eye. "Goodnight," he said again, and left.

Araceli was speechless. But they were so young, she thought, so young! Where were the girl's parents? Surely, they were not yet married. She scanned the long, bony fingers—a habit that had possessed her in her old age—and was relieved to find no ring.

The girl peered at Fortuna, who had settled back down to sleep. The girl's eyes were small and swollen, as if she had had either little or too much sleep. Her cheeks looked dull and yellow.

"Manang's blood transfusion was yesterday," Araceli offered. "We're hoping to be cleared by tomorrow, so we can go home. Is Dr Lim your doctor too?"

"Yes," the girl replied, smiling politely. She looked so small and thin and yellow. Like Manang, Araceli thought, always so frail and sickly. Araceli herself had always been round and healthy.

The Patient

"We come all the way from Pampanga," Araceli continued. "We've been made to stay because Manang's cell count is too low. I hope we can go home by tomorrow."

The girl nodded. It occurred to Araceli that maybe the girl wished to be home as well. Trining cleared her throat beside her, so Araceli returned to the business of making leaves. After a while, she looked up again to check on the girl.

The girl had been watching, her small black eyes blinking and fighting off sleep. "You do that well," she said softly, pointing at a leaf in Araceli's hand.

A short laugh escaped Araceli's lips before she remembered Trining. "Have you eaten?" she asked, slowly sliding off the bed. She took the bag of puto and offered it.

"No, no, thank you."

"You need it, hija, you need to fatten up a bit." Trining had said it pleasantly, but the mother's command in it was unmistakable.

Both Araceli and the girl paused. "I … I really can't … thank you," the girl said. Visibly, she swallowed. "Thank you, but I can't eat. Each time I do—well, I can't keep the food in my stomach."

"Oh dear, but what is the matter with you?"

"Celi," Trining said. "Stop chatting away like that. Can't you see it takes so much effort for the poor girl to speak?"

The girl looked flustered, embarrassed perhaps, to witness such an old woman scolded. Well, there's a comfort, Araceli thought wryly. Some things never change. Even after all these years, I am still Trining's little sister.

Just then the cellphone emitted a melody that sounded vaguely familiar, a popular tune perhaps that she had heard played several times on the radio during past jeepney rides. Araceli was amazed to hear it—a tinny-sounding version of it—come from a phone.

"I guess," the girl was saying, with her hand cupped around the mouthpiece, "I'm missing the first few days of school. Please, will you go to UP for me and talk to all my teachers? My mother can't leave Puerto until the next day."

By the time the girl put her phone away, Araceli could no longer refrain from asking, "You're from UP?" She avoided looking in Trining's direction.

The girl nodded.

"I used to study there myself, but way back when," she laughed. "I'm so old!"

The girl smiled indulgently. Encouraged, Araceli continued, "I took Education. I wanted to be a teacher. In 1968, the campus—"

The girl's gaze slid from Araceli to the movement on her left. Araceli was startled to find Trining standing by the door.

The Patient

"You must be tired, hija," Trining said gently. "Why don't you take my place at the sofa, Celi? I'll sleep with Manang tonight." She waited as Araceli, surprised into silence by the sudden generosity, walked to the sofa. Then the room snapped into darkness.

Araceli lay quiet, first looking out the window between the beds at the little bit of sky beyond, then at the wall above her, where she could trace the faint outline of the window's shadow. She could hear Trining putting their things away, the girl shifting slowly in her bed, then the spasmodic thrummings of the air conditioner. Their room was too far from East Avenue for them to hear the sounds of traffic, but she could imagine the buses there, some of which, she knew, would drive past UP.

She had wasted no more than a year after her mother's death when, at the age of twenty-seven, she had run off to UP. By then her father, weakened by grief as much as old age, had had lighter arms, no longer able to hug and hold her and make her stay.

* *

It had suddenly come to mind, the image of Trining waiting for her in Mrs Valenzuela's sala. Araceli had just finished at the canteen where she worked at night, for pocket money. For tuition, the Americans had kindly provided her with a scholarship to learn how to teach English to Filipino children. She had just let herself in at the gate, had seen the light in the living room through the window and the front door's screen, and had known at once that a visitor had arrived. Visitors often sat in Mrs Valenzuela's sala, usually with one or the other of the lady boarders, as the sala was the first and last room any visitor—gentleman or lady—could be. But no one had ever visited with Araceli yet.

Araceli had just been there some two weeks, had just claimed her scholarship money and enrolled at the College of Education, had just finished a week at the canteen and attended her first class. Everything had shone bright with promise before her, and then suddenly there was Trining. Trining's frown, Trining's tilt of the head, Trining's bearing—a commanding and heavy figure at the age of twenty-eight, having already given birth to four.

At the sight of her, Araceli took a step back into the doorway just as the screen door swung shut. Metal rasped against the skin of her arm. Trining lifted her chin and turned away. Araceli could only show herself to a seat, slip her arm out of her shoulder bag, and remove her bandana, as quietly, inconspicuously, and inoffensively as she could. There was no sign of Mrs Valenzuela anywhere.

Oh, had not Araceli expected that one of her family would come to try and take her home again one day? She had wished

The Patient

for Fortuna, the eldest and the one who should therefore be in charge, but then Manang was known to be too kind, too giving, too gentle. Ah, the logical choice for dealing with miscreants had always been Trining.

Araceli steeled herself. She set her hands slowly upon the arms of her chair, and gripped them tightly. The wood was cool and reassuring, then turned warm and damp soon after Trining began talking. "Well, Celi, you must think yourself very clever, finding this decent establishment for yourself."

She tried to keep things civil and pleasant. "Yes, isn't this a homey place? It really is very comfortable, and ... and conducive to study. Have you—" and her voice broke a bit—"have you seen the campus yet?"

But Trining ignored the question, refused to look at her, and carried on with wounded dignity, "So you're comfortable here, ah yes. And have you thought of our father's comfort, for example, or of your family's. We were all very worried when we found that you had run away from home."

"I did not run away from home ... I asked Tatay!" She found her voice rising in protest, all the while imagining her father and Fortuna's worries. But Trining? It had been easier to imagine Trining cursing her, thinking her foolish and an ingrate. Perhaps she really was one, for what she had done was to pack up all her things before letting herself in her father's room, sitting on his bed, and whispering in his ear, "Tatay, I am leaving for a while, to go to university. Auntie Binay will take care of you while I am away."

It had not been the best arrangement, their old maid aunt almost needing special care herself, but Fortuna and Trining still lived in the same neighborhood after all, and so were within reach. Let them take care of Tatay for a while. And her father had agreed, had placed her hand in his, had merely whispered back, "Come home soon."

Trining let the silence settle around them before finally tugging at her purple blouse and smoothing her long white skirt with her hands. Her hands had remained fair, but had become thick and rough and dry. "Well, Celi, why don't you end this foolishness at once before something disastrous happens? You know that Fortuna and I both have our families to care for; you can't possibly expect us to look after Tatay as well?"

"But, Auntie Binay—"

"Use your head, Celi, what then in an emergency?"

So their arguments had gone, back and forth, back and forth. And Araceli, despite knowing that it would happen one day, was ill-prepared for the confrontation. Still, she stuck to her choices as firmly as she stuck to her chair, gripping the armrests more and more tightly. She lost track of all her

The Patient

arguments, one link in the chain unraveling after another. She found herself in tears, getting more and more hysterical in the face of Trining's stillness and composure, increasingly shamefaced when she saw the lady boarders peer at her from the curtains that separated the dining room from the living room, and mortified when Mrs Valenzuela finally walked through a part in the curtains with her arms crossed and her gaze disapproving.

"Is everything alright, ladies?"

Trining stood up then and extended her hand to Mrs Valenzuela, who took it. "Everything is fine, Mrs Valenzuela," she said evenly, speaking to an equal. "I just wanted a word with my sister, and now we are done." And then, as a parting shot, she leaned over and kissed Araceli on her forehead, saying, "Very well, Celi, have it your way."

Araceli had then had her wish to remain in UP—nobody had come to get her since—but that night, she had been wrung like a rag, and had felt that she had lost. She had not known what to say to Mrs Valenzuela except, "I'm sorry, this will not happen again," before bursting into another round of tears and rushing to her bed, forgetting her handbag and bandana in the sala. And then she could not bear to get it, to join the boarders at dinner that night, could not stand to see—as she imagined—looks of recrimination and reproach. All the giggling and secret sharing that evening, in the evenings that followed, suddenly had to do with her. And yet somebody had been her friend, and left her bag and bandana at the foot of her bed, for her to find when she awoke.

Mrs Valenzuela had remained distant and non-committal, although Araceli felt sure she was all black marks in Mrs Valenzuela's book. And yet surprisingly, year after year, Mrs Valenzuela renewed her contract and allowed her to stay.

∽ ∾

Araceli woke with a crick in her neck and a fog in her brain. She lay unable to move, trying to get her bearings, before she thought to open her eyes and look around her. First she saw the tray table where lay the patients' plate-covered breakfasts, and then a nurse changing the IV bottle of the young girl across Manang's bed. Then she remembered she had been given the sofa, and realized she had not made the most of it. She had not stretched herself upon it, and rested, but instead had let her mind wander back in time. It was like walking several miles in the heat and dust. As she eased herself slowly into a sitting position, she felt her whole body cry out complaints. Retirement had finally made her old.

"Araceli," Fortuna called in a crackling whisper, then raised a weak and withered arm towards the breakfast.

The Patient

Under one plate she found steamed fish and steamed rice, with boiled egg. For the younger patient, no doubt, Araceli thought wryly, for she had forgotten to pack Manang's teeth. How was she to know, having just moved back to Pampanga? She winced as she remembered Trining's stream of reprimands, which had finally driven her out of the room and into the hospital's chapel the day before. And she, if only Trining had known, a non-practicing Catholic!

To Fortuna she brought the steaming bowl of lugaw. She placed it upon Manang's stomach, knowing the warmth would be comforting, then gently cranked the upper half of the hospital bed so that it rose and helped Fortuna to a sitting position. Trining emerged from the bathroom, all bathed and ready for the day, just as Araceli was about to feed her elder sister.

"You forgot to wash your hands again, Celi," she said, then took Fortuna's bowl of lugaw away from her. "Let me do it while you freshen up."

Araceli went without a word, and if Trining thought that she had done so in quick obedience, then she was wrong. For Araceli had suddenly felt a strong wave of resentment sweeping through her, and quickly, she had to bury it, under the great big pail in the shower, or, let it trickle down the drain.

139

At her father's deathbed, she had felt the same stormy anger towards Trining. Nobody else had had the inclination to write her other than Trining, and Araceli had withstood all the many underhanded ways Trining used to make her feel guilty just so she could have news of her family.

Tatay sends his love, and would write you in his own hand, except that he is now terribly weak. He seems terribly lonely, with no other person but Auntie Binay to keep him company.

Araceli had gritted her teeth, and addressed her letters not only to Trining, but to her father, to Manang Fortuna, and to Auntie Binay. She wrote about her training as an educator, and of the children in classes that, for her practicum, she had the opportunity to teach. She mentioned the Literature, Philosophy, and History majors she had befriended, their trips to the Museo, the National Library, the zoo, and the bay in Manila. And she refused to let any sign of her missing them show.

You should see the state of your home now, left to disrepair and decay. Auntie Binay is too slow to keep abreast of things. Shouldn't you perhaps spend a summer here and have all the odds and ends attended to before our home comes tumbling down? It is all we will have left of Papa and Mama.

The Patient

She no doubt could have found the time and saved the money for a trip back to Pampanga in the summer, but she had been too frightened of Trining's long arm. If Trining's hand could keep her at a stranglehold, all the way in Diliman, then at close range in Pampanga, she could suffocate and never be allowed to return. And then one day, some weeks into her senior year, she had been forced to take the trip.

Tatay is dying, Celi, and perhaps you are the only one left that he needs to bid goodbye before he passes away. You have no right to keep him away from his Creator any longer. For his sake, if not for ours, please come home.

The devious Trining had finally hit upon the right set of words to make her not only come home, but rush home. Daily she had cried with guilt and remorse over her father's body, as it grew smaller and more withered. Her father, unable to speak without extreme effort, just quietly looked at her, with what she interpreted to be love and forgiveness in his eyes. He would let her hold his hand, and from time to time, he would smile, sigh, and fall peacefully asleep. It had taken all of one month before she discovered that she had been tricked.

One day, as she paid the carpenter his wages for fixing her doors, the unevenness of her dressers and tables, the shutters on her windows, the corrugated metal sheet on her roof, and the endless other things that he had been tasked, and had tasked himself, to do, he said, "Now that all is good and strong again, you can invite your sisters and their families, and have a proper party."

"Oh yes," Auntie Binay agreed, "and now that Manong Francisco seems to be on the mend again, we should celebrate, Celi."

She looked from the carpenter to her aunt, and then everything she had not noticed in the midst of her grief added up all at once in her mind—how her sisters' visits had dwindled as she had taken more upon herself to care for her father; how the people in the streets, the people in the market, the people who did service in her house, had asked after her father without any sign of sympathy or pity for her; how the priest had come every Sunday to give him communion, but did not always stay long enough for confession; and how the doctor had paid them only one visit, and that was to leave a prescription for more medicine with Auntie Binay. Perhaps she at first thought that nobody outside of her family knew that her father was dying; perhaps she thought that the doctor had simply given up on her father; but with time to think: how could a small town not know what was happening? How could the doctor, who was her father's friend, not come more often?

Her first impulse had been to rush to her room and get all her bags packed as soon as possible, but the moment she saw

The Patient

her school things, she remembered that she had already missed too many weeks of classes, and so had to wait for the next semester.

Trining may have been surprised the next time she came to visit and Araceli gave her the cold shoulder. But she had too much dignity to address it, and pretended not to notice. Everybody else had. Auntie Binay one day observed that "Manong Francisco would not want his family fighting over inheritance, you know, Celi, especially while he is still alive." And Manang Fortuna cornered her in church one Sunday and asked, "What malice has Trining ever done you, Celi? She can be terribly stern, I know, but has she not watched over you and written you and advised you all the time you were at university?"

Araceli had her own pride, and kept her silence. Besides, how was she to explain the damage that Trining had wrought upon her life? If she had been blamed for breaking her father's heart and making him sicken and die, then she would have blamed Trining for doing the very same thing to her. If only Trining had waited a minute, a day, a month, before sending off her false, traitorous letter. But she had not, so Araceli had died before her father ever even drew his last breath.

Through the mirror in the bathroom, while she combed her hair, Araceli watched the young girl stir in her sleep. Her eyes blinked drowsily a few times before they focused on the boy in front of her. She smiled and accepted the yellow rose he offered, but he had to help her put it down again on the table beside her. When he indicated her uneaten breakfast, she shook her head. He did not insist, and once again smoothed her hair away from her face and kissed her tenderly upon her forehead.

"Why are you smiling?" Trining asked her, as she folded her towel once and hung it on the back of the sofa. There was no other place for it.

Araceli shrugged and busied herself with picking a crochet needle and a piece of green thread.

"Try to do them right this time," Trining advised, and Araceli merely nodded, biting her tongue on the retort that by being right or proper all the time, one missed out on many things in the world. Many times, at university, Araceli had heard Trining's voice in her head, and gleefully disobeyed. By talking to strangers in the canteen where she worked, and at the library where she studied, she had met people who had then become her friends, who had introduced her to more people, until she had many different groups of people she could go with on weekend trips. True, she had been ten years older than most of them, but it had been a source of thrill for her, and for them, to find out when the next new friend would discover the fact. Some took the first few minutes upon meeting, while others took days, or even weeks. Alfredo had taken weeks.

"Hepatitis, Ma'am," the young man said.

Araceli looked up just in time to see Fortuna withdrawing an arm. No doubt she had pointed at the girl to ask what was ailing her. Araceli had not heard Trining scold Manang; Trining had always found fault with only one sister, and hardly ever the other.

"Hepatitis! But how—"

"Celi, you are making it too tight again, see?" Trining had taken the leaf that was taking form in her hand and had laid it upon the table. Again, it did not lie flat.

As she unraveled the thread, she noticed the young man looking at her. When she smiled at him, he said, "Nobody knows how she got it. Usually hepatitis comes from eating dirty food, but there's an incubation period of one to two weeks."

"Ah," Araceli said, beginning the leaf again. He reminded her of many of her students through the years, so earnest-looking as they stood in front of the class for their book reports. "So there's no way to trace the disease to a particular day, to a particular thing."

He nodded. "And we eat out sometimes. We're dormers, you see."

Trining stood up abruptly and said, "Well, perhaps I should see about our lunch. What should we have?"

"Let's try the pizza," Araceli suggested.

"Too much cheese," Trining grabbed her leather handbag. "I'll just get what I find, okay?"

She turned to the young man, who held up his hands and shook his head. "No, thank you," he said. Araceli smiled. For a moment he had looked as if he were fending off an attack.

When Trining left, Araceli hummed a little made-up tune. From the corner of her eye, she watched the young man sit himself more comfortably on the bed at the girl's feet and look at her solemnly. He picked up a foot and tickled it tentatively. The girl laughed. Fortuna opened her eyes and smiled.

"So, where are you from?" Araceli asked.

"She's from Puerto Princesa," he said, promptly letting go of the foot. "I'm from Baguio."

"Ah," Araceli said again, and decided that perhaps she had better just attend to her leaves and leave the two lovebirds alone. Leaves, leave, leaving, left. Gone. She bit her lip and shook her head.

The Patient

Alfredo had also come from Baguio. He had always eaten his lunch and dinner at the canteen where she worked. She had always been quite frightened of him, of his unkempt hair, his loud voice, his willowy tallness, the faded pair of pants he always wore. He would tell her later on that they had belonged to his father, who had been in the military, and had died in the line of duty. Before then, however, for almost the whole year that she worked at the canteen, she had tried her best to avoid him, had tried to make sure that some other person would be at the counter when he came up to be served.

And then one day, he stood up to leave the table just as she finished closing the counter for the night. "Good night, Manong," she called to the janitor, who was putting up chairs on unoccupied tables. The others were still crowded with students cramming for exams or meeting for group projects. Just as she closed the door, he yanked at it roughly. She cried out as all the books that she had borrowed from the library came tumbling down.

He would swear later on that he had not planned such a dramatic meeting, but from time to time, she doubted it. Alfredo had an artistic bent, a charismatic voice, a flair for the theatric. He admitted that he had fortunately recognized one of the books she dropped; otherwise he would not have known what to say.

"Ah, Rousseau," he said, picking the book up from the floor and dusting it with his shirt. "One whose ideas inspired the French Revolution."

She had not yet known that, for she had not yet opened the book. "Oh … well … I'm researching on his thoughts on education." She immediately felt foolish.

"You should read *Emile*, then. I have a friend, a Literature Major, who has just bought a copy."

And then she had been grateful to him, this rugged History student who had offered to introduce her the next day to the Literature Major. She had thought then, walking home, that for all his height and scruffiness, he was a harmless man after all. She had, of course, thought wrong.

∽ ∾

She had nodded off. The smell of fried chicken filled her nose, the sound of crackling plastic filled her ears. Trining was just about to put down a Styrofoam container of Chicken Joy beside her. Behind Trining, the girl was in the process of getting up. The young man helped with a hand at her elbow, while a nurse held up the IV bottle, making sure the long winding tube was out of the way. An attendant waited with a wheelchair just a few steps away.

The Patient

"They've found a private room for her," Trining mumbled. "Just as well. We're due to leave this afternoon. I checked at the desk."

Araceli nodded, attempting to clear her mind and to focus on the young couple. They seemed to be a long way off. When she stood up to stretch, the young man smiled at her.

"Goodbye," the young girl said softly.

"You take care of yourself now," Araceli found herself saying, surprised by her own motherly voice. "Get well soon," and then she was winking. She had often taken the jolly, grandmotherly role with her students in her later years of teaching.

"Thanks," the girl replied, and the young man smiled again.

As the attendant wheeled them out of the room, Araceli felt a wave of despair wash through her. She wanted to call out, "Keep well, the two of you," but for what? What did well-wishing do in the course of unswerving fate?

Trining's voice broke into her thoughts. "Our lunch is still hot. Would you like some, Manáng?"

They shared a little of their food with Fortuna, who was not very hungry. They knew, however, that hospital food would tempt her even less.

"When we get home to Pampanga," Trining said, "the first thing I am going to do is check on my little apos."

Home. To Pampanga. She had not thought of Pampanga as her home for the longest time. "I shall have to continue unpacking all my stuff. Your getting sick was actually a pleasant break for me, Manang."

Fortuna smiled indulgently.

Trining sighed and shook her head. "They're not that young anymore, I know, but still, I can't help but think of them as little children. I suppose Jun could even have a girlfriend by now, without ever having told us. They just start younger and younger these days, don't they?"

Araceli had no doubt where that thought had come from. It was funny, the way they compared the youth of today with their own; how they registered shock whenever faced with young love, how young, how young, when they themselves had been expected to marry before they turned twenty.

"You would think they could have been more considerate knowing there were other people in the room," Trining said.

"Oh, I think they looked sweet," Araceli said.

"You and your romantic notions," Trining scoffed, and absentmindedly shoved the book *Little Women* forward. Araceli waited. It used to be that Trining would then link her romantic notions with never having married—"There is no Mr Right; look at you, wasted all your time by waiting for him"—but it seemed that Trining had lost her bite. Araceli picked up the

The Patient

book, and looked for the page where she had stopped. She remembered now that she had also studied this book in connection with the writer's father, Bronson Alcott, and his ideas on education. She had dreamed then of putting up her own little school based on her own ideas, and Alfredo had laughed at her naïveté. She had forgiven him his cruel remarks, because he had offered them with a hug and a kiss on her forehead.

"Shouldn't we start packing, Araceli? Once we're packed—"

Araceli stood up and brought out the sports bag from under the bed. As usual, their packing consisted of Araceli doing most of the physical work, while Trining looked up from time to time from her rosary work to make comments and give orders. As Araceli cleared the table of their accumulated pile of Styrofoam, plastic spoons and forks and bags, Trining stopped her and inspected what could be washed and salvaged. "No, Trining," Araceli decided, "let's just throw these all away. We can't possibly take them all to Pampanga with us."

"But what a waste!" Trining protested.

Araceli placed them all on the table again, then turned to her sister. "You can wash them, if you like, and then pack them yourself."

Trining looked taken aback, but Araceli pressed her lips together and turned away. She knew both Fortuna and Trining were looking at her, so, strode to the door. "I'll be right back," she called in the silence, without looking back.

∽ ∾

One youngish woman in her thirties sat in the pew nearest the altar. Araceli hesitated by the Chapel door, then decided that silent company with a stranger was much more preferable than the company of Trining at the moment. She sat herself at the last pew, across the aisle and diagonally opposite the woman.

Despite the Chapel's white walls, and the wooden altar's white tablecloth, the room had a dimness about it. Natural light came faintly through the windows above, near the ceiling. The fluorescent lights were not in use, only the two electric candles on either side of the altar, giving off a faint red glow that lit up the nailed feet of the Christ on the cross. Araceli smirked and closed her eyes again, trying not to picture the bag of blood that had flowed and emptied into Fortuna the day before.

She remembered the first time that Alfredo had tried to convince her that there was no God, that God was just some kind of construct, some kind of "opium" with which to keep the poor content with their lot. How had he phrased it again? All she could remember clearly now was how he had looked, full of gestures and fists and flashing eyes, wild and earnest and fiery with her as he had been in front of hundreds of students who had attended one or the other of his many demonstrations. She had always thought of the demonstrations as "his," whereas he had not even been one of the organization's officers, just one of its most eloquent and convincing speakers.

He never succeeded in convincing her. She had simply regarded it as one of the quirks of his youth, one of the necessary phases that an educated man might go through. He had, after all, been ten years younger than her, like all the rest of their friends, and she had often wondered if perhaps that was why he liked her; she could have been another kind of rebellion to him, and something he had quite conquered.

If only she could have also turned it around, but he had never been hers alone. Even in their most intimate moments, his hand in hers, her head on his chest, his pointed chin nesting in her hair, he would talk of how enlightened young people like himself could change the way of education, the way of government, and the way of the world. He had thrilled her sometimes, dreaming out loud about living simply, in some mountain or other, where they could raise and educate their children away from the grime and the malice of the city. But then he would go back to talking about the city, how it might still be reformed, how they could all still make a difference.

She had loved it all, his youth and his idealism, his dreams of a better future. She had indulged him each time he wanted to speak, she had plied him with questions and tried to poke holes in his arguments, all the while waiting and waiting with bated breath for him to hug her close, kiss her on her forehead, and mention once more their home in the mountains, their simple life, their children. Perhaps even her schoolhouse.

And then one day, he had gone off to the mountains without her, along with his student group instead of her. There appeared bits and pieces of it in the radio, of demonstrations in Malacañang, of a student rampage, of arrests and brutality and guns. She could barely piece it all together, and could find no clue as to why he would leave without telling her, why he would leave her all alone. Once again, she refused to eat supper with the other boarders, even when finally Mrs Valenzuela herself came to call her to the table. She attended Mass each day, and prayed each and every night, for her to forgive him, for him to come back, and finally, just for him to be safe.

God had answered her prayers then; it was something she could have told Alfredo, had she the presence of mind. But in the middle of the night, heavy with sleep, she was shaken roughly, with whispers that burned her ear. Alfredo had broken into Mrs Valenzuela's boarding house for ladies, and was leaning close to her and grasping at her hands. "Come with me," he said ... perhaps he had even pleaded.

She had half-risen, she was going, she embraced him, then smelled the soil and the sweat on him, and something else—was it blood? Was he hurt?

And then he pushed her back into her pillow with a grimy hand, "No, I'm a wanted man. It's not safe. You could get hurt." His hand lingered near her heart, and she struggled to stand up, the image of a simple life in her mind. "It will be a rough life," he said, as if reading her thoughts. "And we can't have a family."

Only then did she remember her own family, and Trining's letter, received just that day, summoning her home to her father's deathbed. She had wept, and he held her and kissed her repeatedly on her lips, so that his beard scratched her face. She ran her hands through his tangled hair. And then he asked for her address in Pampanga, so she whispered it to him three or four times, over and over, so that he could memorize it. He held her tightly one last time, wiped her eyes and smoothed her hair back, and kissed her on her forehead.

And then the long wait in Pampanga, through the wasted semester and through that cold-shoulder spell with Trining. She heard on the radio that an amnesty had been declared, and thus expected to hear from him each morning, perhaps to even see him come running up the driveway and knocking boldly on her door. She kept imagining with delight Trining's disbelief and her father's blessings. If only Trining had given her another minute, another day, another month, before sending her false letter, then perhaps things would have turned out differently.

And then, as if to prove Trining right after all, her father died, clutching at her hand one last time on his deathbed, before shuddering into a sleep he would never wake from again. They had to wait for Fortuna to come home from the United States, on a business trip with her husband, before they could bury their father, a week into the second semester. She had to miss that semester as well, had to attend to a thousand and one details that her father and Auntie Binay had failed to mind, had to turn her mind away from thoughts of Alfredo in school, waiting for her in vain, and perhaps, just perhaps, bumping into another girl and making her books tumble to the ground. She stopped praying then.

When she finally went back to school the next year, she found no sign of Alfredo. None of her old friends could tell where he had gone, and the student organization had been disbanded. On a trip to Baguio, all they discovered was a photograph of his father in a yearbook at the PMA, looking very much like him, with dark eyes and a mischievous smirk

The Patient

to his mouth. She still hoped each morning that he would finally show up, all through her student life, through her training at a nearby grade school, through her first job there as well. And then she learned to forget, to shun other men, and devote her life to city children who were not her own, but whom she loved for their youth and their idealism. Alfredo had never convinced her that there was no God, but her own life had shown her that even if there were one, it didn't very much matter.

༄ ༄

A young man walked past her and greeted the woman in front before genuflecting by the altar. Araceli recognized him as the priest who had said Mass the evening before. Perhaps now there was going to be an afternoon Mass. She leaned back on her chair and waited, closing her eyes and breathing deeply. Ah, she could just sink into blessed sleep here.

Here I am, she thought wryly, driven back to you without choice by that bully, my sister. But as you can see, I no longer need another month, another day, not even another minute.

'THE ABOMINABLE SNOWMAN'

The Abominable Snowman

When Sammie woke up, he saw at once that it had begun to snow. He thought at first that he was dreaming, or that Mount Pinatubo had erupted again and was showering Manila with a generous amount of ash, but when he slid his window open and stuck his hand out, a genuine snowflake came to rest on his palm, tickling a spot momentarily with an icy tingle. He remembered his Social Studies teacher in grade five, who had asked, "How many of you would like the Philippines to be a colony of the United States?" Only a few had raised their hands, Sammie included, and the teacher had zeroed in on him and demanded, "Why?" He had replied, "So that we can have snow!"

If that had only happened nearer this day, he would have been saved from two minutes of cruel laughter and two years of humiliation. His classmates had never stopped teasing him about it, calling him "Sammie the Snowman." His round face and belly, his sausage-like arms and legs, his beady black eyes and thick black hair, didn't help one bit. On the bulletin board, where the photo prints of the class were posted, and under which students signed on pieces of paper for their individual orders, someone had drawn a top hat on Sammie's head with a thick black marker. This was repeated in every shot, and in one, someone had added a dot on his nose with a red pen.

Sammie sighed, then realized with a start that his face was beginning to get crusty with snow. He turned away from the window and took one last look at his bed. This was too precious a morning to waste on the making of beds. He thundered down the stairs, causing his mother to scold from the kitchen. "Hoy, Samson, can you please keep quiet or you'll wake—" Desi, his baby sister, bawled on cue. Sammie dashed out the front door before his mother could order him back up the stairs to get her.

The nine year-old twins from next door grinned at the sight of him. They were dressed in matching Levis and Nikes, although one wore a red long-sleeved sweater and the other a green one. Sammie ignored their pointed looks at his shorts, coming loose at the garter, and his favorite white t-shirt, now quite gray and frayed at the collar. He didn't much care, and didn't feel too cold. He threw back his head and threw out his arms as if to embrace the sky, then spun a clumsy turn before

The Abominable Snowman

falling to the snow-dusted sidewalk. The snow was coming quite thickly now; he smiled at the thought of being covered in it, like being under the sand at a beach.

He heard the twins snicker. In high school that was what the teasing had dwindled into—a snicker here and there behind a book or binder, a nudge of an elbow or a lift of an eyebrow as he passed, or a comic imitation of himself lumbering behind him. He had grown the inches that would match his stoutness, changing the word "fat" or "obese" to the word "huge." He had also been invited to join the basketball team, something that would have raised him in the estimation of his peers, except that after he failed Math and English in his first year, the coach kicked him out. At the very worst, a smart aleck would suddenly invite Sammie to partake of chocolate-covered macadamia nuts, or to put on somebody's new pair of Cole Haan shoes, saying, "Try this, pare, it's stateside!" And another would say, "Oh no, baka mag-snow!" But nobody ever called him "Sammie the Snowman" to his face, like they constantly did in grade school. It had become easier to stop them too, by suddenly standing up and pushing a chair away so that it grated on the floor. They would stop, at least, until after he walked out the door.

He stood up quickly, so that flakes of snow fell off him and scattered on the sidewalk. The twins turned on their heels and ran shrieking until they reached their gate. Sammie didn't stir. He looked down at the loose shape he had made surrounded by little mounds of snow, beginning to whiten, fade, and disappear.

∽ ∾

Mrs Inocencio didn't notice the snow at first. She had had no time to look out the window, not since she had woken thirty minutes later than she had instructed her alarm clock, and cooked breakfast for her demanding family. At the kitchen table, Mr Inocencio shut off the world even as he digested its news, with newspaper raised in front of him. She worried that his bacon and eggs would get cold, but each time she urged him to eat, he flicked the newspaper before obliging. He had flicked it quite violently when Sammie raced down the stairs just a moment ago. Then she rushed to get Desi, because Sammie hadn't heard her request to bring his sister down, and because the newspaper was in danger of being flicked to pieces before Mrs Inocencio could ever hope to read it. And finally there was Ferdie, the middle child, scrawny and slow, chewing his mouthful thirty times before ever remembering to swallow. She had to keep encouraging him to try another bite. If she left him on his own, then he would be in time for school the next morning, but never today.

Finally Mrs Inocencio brought Ferdie and his father to the door, kissing them both on their cheeks as she let them out. And then all three of them paused at the cold nip of air

The Abominable Snowman

and at the sight of millions of tiny, feathery bits swirling beyond their doorstep.

Ferdie, slow one though he was, found his tongue first. "I thought it was snow. It IS snow."

Mr and Mrs Inocencio looked at each other over his head.

"There was nothing in the newspaper?" Mrs Inocencio finally asked.

Mr Inocencio, after a pause, took Ferdie by the shoulders. "I think you should stay home. Obey mommy, okay?"

"Hooray!" he cried, and squirmed free of his father's grasp. He waddled off to the kitchen, no doubt bound to kiss or torment his little sister sitting on her high chair, yelling for "Maaaa."

"This isn't possible," Mr Inocencio told his wife.

"Bring a jacket," Mrs Inocencio told her husband.

Mr Inocencio shrugged. "I got one in the office. I'm late. Tell the good-for-nothing he stays home two days, but he either has to go back to school or get a job. There will be no slacking in this house."

Mrs Inocencio knew whom he meant, but had no time to brood on either Sammie or the snow until after she had fed Desi her Cerelac and parked both Ferdie and Desi in front of the TV and Cartoon Network. She watched the first few minutes of Courage the Cowardly Dog with them before she went to the kitchen sink to do the dishes and look out the window. Several people in the neighborhood had already discovered the snowfall, just as they had. There were Miss Martinez and her recently widowed Aunt, wrapped in jackets sensible enough for Baguio weather, making their first tentative steps out of their house across the street. There were four of the Nemesio children huddled over a mound of snow, making the first-ever snowballs of their lives. There were the Garcia twins next door, warmly dressed and looking like Christmas, joining them and starting the first snowball fight on the street. And there was Mrs Garcia, resplendent in a fur coat that had certainly never been used in these islands before.

She had been looking slightly to her right to see all of them. When she looked left, she caught sight of her husband, still out there in his car, yelling something across the death seat and out the car window at Sammie, who was looking down at the ground and scuffing at the snow with a bare foot. She grew angry at once, and rushed to the front door. "Samson, get in here, you mindless boy. You'll catch your death like that, standing out there in the cold—"

"Maaaa," Desi called from the sala.

"Mommy?" Ferdie called too, with less certainty.

Sammie stood, still with head bowed, even as Mr Inocencio finished yelling his piece and drove off. "Samson!" she commanded, and when he didn't move, she pleaded, "Sammie…" He raised his head then, looking at the playing

The Abominable Snowman

children first before he looked at her. She saw little particles of snow glinting in his hair, on his eyebrows, his cheeks, his arms and his feet. Perhaps she even saw some on his eyelashes, although she couldn't remember Sammie ever having eyelashes. When she met his eyes, she almost staggered back with the thought that she no longer knew her son, but she steeled herself and stretched out a hand to him. He backed away then, and ran off, away from the children, and down the street.

"Sammie?" she called. "Sam?"

The children outside took up her cry. "Sam Sam Sammie? Sam Sam Sammie?" they chanted. She saw Mrs Garcia look her up and down and quickly shut the door, adjusting the straps of her housedress before she went to her bedroom to put on a sweater and get jackets for her little ones. Sammie could very well take care of himself; perhaps he had run to that friend of his on the next street, what was his name, that only son of Mrs Haw's. Back in the living room, she quickly put Desi into her jacket, then helped Ferdie with his. Desi clung to her right shoulder, and Ferdie tried to follow suit with her left. On TV, an old woman in spectacles hugged Courage the Cowardly Dog. Mrs Inocencio turned to hug her children. When she finally took her place at the kitchen sink again, she saw that the children outside had begun to build a snowman.

Mr Inocencio punched at the buttons of his Kenwood, searching for a station with news of the sudden snow. He had quickly gotten used to the idea of snow in the Philippines, or, perhaps, for all he knew, only in Manila. Why not in Manila? For a few years now, the weather had been rather screwed up anyway. Rains in October instead of in August, a summer heat during Christmas, so why not an exaggerated cold spell during March? It must have had something to do with the world's depleting ozone or with illegal loggers or something. The environmentalists would have a field day now. At any rate, he needed to get to his office in one piece. He hadn't counted on the roads being rather more slippery than when there were heavy rains. He switched his windshield wipers to high, then went back to search through the channels of his radio.

Rock music and DJs with their American twang abounded. The snow perhaps gave them even more twang, he thought wryly. Somewhere in the 94 area, he snagged on the word "snowing" and stopped his fiddling. From all over the city, people called in about snow in their districts, and what they or their children were doing, or what had happened to their plants or pets or front or back yards.

Something scratched at the back of his mind, some household thought or dilemma that he had meant to leave behind as he drove away from his subdivision. These days he had to be fully focused on work; this late in March they had to

The Abominable Snowman

make some adjustments on the budget, and they had an up-and-coming case in court because some dissatisfied client was suing.

He had been just about to speed up when he saw the traffic ahead. Truck after truck on the second lane, not moving, men in yellow raincoats and black boots waving at cars in the second lane to move to the lanes on either side, other cars in other lanes blaring their horns, not wanting to give way. Mr Inocencio stopped to let a station wagon through, but then an FX immediately skidded in, and then a taxi. He leaned on his horn and stared down the driver of a maroon SUV about to follow the taxi. He swerved slightly to his right to intimidate the driver further, then drove after the taxi, not bothering to keep a safe distance. Mr Inocencio grunted—the idea of give-and-take were lost on these people. Barbarians.

An image of Sammie in his shorts and bare feet flashed in his mind. Mr Inocencio had come across the boy just outside the house, looking down at his arms as it furred up with snow, a blank stupid look on his face. Mr Inocencio couldn't help but yell at him then, to startle him out of his reverie, and to pound some sense into him. Sammie just had to attend the last of his classes and pass his exams, then he could move on to his second year of high school. Why flunk his first year? How difficult could first year be? His eldest son was no quitter, was he? Well he better not quit, or else he better start looking for a job, and he better make up his mind soon. He seemed to believe he could make his own decisions without the help of his father anyway.

Mr Inocencio slammed on his brakes as a crowd with banners and signs came out of a building and poured into the highway. "Repent! It's the end of the world!" "Pray for all souls!" Some women began to dance and twirl in the snow. Mr Inocencio shook his head. Fanatics. Someone had even scrawled on cartolina a couple of lines from Robert Frost's poem: "Some say the world will end in fire, some in ice." He had learned this poem in high school, it had been easy, so simple ... Mr Inocencio gritted his teeth. Of course, he could just transfer Sammie to another school, he didn't want any son of his to be an out-of-school youth. What was he doing, leaving that stupid son of a bitch to make his own decision?

"There are about three accidents down the length of C5," a caller was telling the DJ. "I heard, ha. I'm here on EDSA, but we're stuck here too."

Mr Inocencio groaned. He had chosen to take the EDSA route this morning. He looked absently into the other vehicles around him. He glimpsed two people seemingly talking to themselves, their cellphones out of sight. He reached for his Nokia and began to call his secretary.

∾ ∾

The Abominable Snowman

Danny Haw halfheartedly surfed through the channels of cable TV. He didn't want to admit it, but perhaps going to school would have actually been better than being made to stay home. There had been no announcement from the DECS yet, about classes being cancelled for the day, but as it was, his mother didn't even want him leaving his room. At first watching the NBA on ESPN had entertained him, but he was getting restless.

He threw the remote control down the carpet and gave it a kick for good measure. This made the TV change channel, and now he was glaring at MTV Request. Martian the VJ looked silly wearing a ski cap. Danny turned towards the window in disgust, and lifted a curtain to gaze out. The whole street, snow-covered and completely white, was empty. Even the sky had emptied; the snowing had stopped. He could hear his mother on the phone in the next room, speaking in her flawless Mandarin, no doubt calling every house up and down their road. No kid in a Chinese family was going to be allowed out. He smirked and remembered what his Ate said about the Chinese' Filipinos—how they were believed to be all conservative, all afraid of change, all exclusive. How true these stereotypes sometimes seemed.

And then Danny saw movement, and put a hand on the knob of his window, ready to twist it open and call out. Some Chinese kid had got lucky. As the figure stopped at his gate,

Danny drew breath and took an involuntary step back. This was no Chinese boy out there; it was Sammie Inocencio. From behind his blue curtain, Danny watched as Sammie looked up at the Haws' gate with its green spikes, glinting and beginning to ice. Sammie just stood there in his shorts and shirt and—Danny snorted—without slippers or shoes. Typical Inocencio, stupid stupid stupid.

The bruise in Danny's left side, just below his ribs, began to throb and call attention to itself. Danny tried to ignore it, tried to breathe evenly, all the time keeping his eye on Sammie. What was he doing here? What was he planning to do? Was he looking for another fight?

The bruise throbbed harder, forcing Danny to double over. He lifted his shirt and blew gingerly on the purple splotch that marred his many layers of skin, down to the surface of muscle. He hadn't really meant to anger Sammie, he had just wanted his classmates to laugh. They had been discussing legendary monsters in English class, like Grendel in *Beowulf*, a part of which they were about to take up. "Name some," Miss Tan had said. Had that really been just yesterday?

"Bigfoot." "King Kong." "The Lochness Monster." "Godzilla." "The Abo—The Abomn—The Abo-mi-na-ble Snowman." They had all laughed at how hard it was to pronounce. Even Miss Tan couldn't get it on the first try. Then Danny had yelled, "The what? The Abobomo Snowman?" They

The Abominable Snowman

had laughed harder. He hadn't really meant to, but he had glanced at Sammie then, and laughed. Well, maybe other people had laughed and glanced at Sammie too. He didn't know. All he could remember was watching Sammie. Who hadn't been laughing. Who had been looking around with that stupid expression on his face. Who had suddenly stood up and wrapped an arm around Danny, and then punched him over and over again with a balled up fist, right in the same spot, over and over again.

Danny winced. He could still remember his own face turning cold, the moment Sammie stood up and his chair scraped the floor. He could still remember backing away the moment he realized Sammie had grown ten feet tall, about to attack him. He was no coward, he had tried to fight back, really, but Sammie had been like a UFC champion, keeping him in a stranglehold until all he could do was scream.

Danny peered out the window again. Sammie still stood there, studying his arms as he stretched them out. His left foot swung rhythmically, scuffling at the snow.

Miss Tan had ordered them both to present themselves at the principal's office, after Sammy had refused to apologize and Danny had refused to go to the clinic. Their parents had been called. Sammie's mother had arrived first. She could drive on her own. Danny's mother must have had to wait for the driver to come from his father's office building. Danny remembered thinking this as he listened for his mother's arrival, and waited his turn to be interviewed by the principal. He could hear them inside, because the secretary had failed to shut the door completely, and Danny sat right by it.

"But that isn't like Sammie." Mrs Inocencio had said. "They're friends. They're busmates. They're neighbors."

Mrs Inocencio and Danny's mother could have driven over together.

"Smammie," Sammie's baby sister had added.

Mrs Inocencio had had to bring the baby with her. They had no maids.

The principal had spoken in a lower voice. Danny could barely hear him. "You will be suspended for two days."

As they came out of the office, he heard Sammie tell his mother, "I am never going back to school."

Danny's mother could not make it. She had called the secretary, and had not even asked to speak to Danny. The secretary had to tell him that his mother could not come.

Danny yanked at the window and stuck his head out, shaking a fist in the chill. He cried involuntarily at the pain that tore at his side, but he was no coward. Sammie looked up, having heard the strange sound that Danny had made. Danny screamed at the top of his lungs, "Snowman! Abobomo Snowman!" He screamed until his mother came to his side,

The Abominable Snowman

trying to get hold of him, trying to shake him. When he looked down into the street again, Sammie had disappeared.

∽ ∾

The Garcia twins yearned to get back to their snowman. They had formed his body with a huge ball and with a medium-sized ball. They had left the Nemesio children in charge of the head.

"Make it as huge as a basketball," Mikko had instructed.

"We'll be back later with the eyes and nose," Martin had said.

They had wanted to stay but Mrs Garcia had called them in to lunch. Now, because it had begun to snow again, their mother refused to allow them outside until they wore warmer stuff.

"This is enough, mom," Mikko said, tugging at his red sweater.

"No," their mother said, flitting around the guest room from one balikbayan box to another in her beige fur coat. "We don't know when it'll stop snowing for good."

"Mom, puhlease!" Martin said, jiggling the black buttons in his hand. He wanted to be the one to give the snowman eyes. Mikko had the nose in his pocket, which was a carrot he had charmed from their cook.

"I said wait. Your parkas are here somewhere."

They had worn those bulky things on their trip to the US last Christmas, to pay their father's older brother and his family a visit. They had been grateful for the warmth then, as they always spent their time outdoors being taught by their cousins how to snowboard and make snow angels. But now wearing parkas in Manila only seemed absurd.

"Mom—" Mikko began, but stopped when their mother straightened to her full height. They were two boys, and she was just a girl, but she was taller. And if they ran out, she could tell their houseboy Dondon to get them and not let them out again. They were wise to her punishing ways.

Martin nudged Mikko to the window. When they both looked out, all they could see was a part of the roof over the first floor, and then the empty lot across the street. The roof blocked their view of the snowman.

Mikko and Martin stood among the balikbayan boxes their mother had not yet bothered to unpack. The bed, completely surrounded by these boxes, had already disappeared under pillows vacuum-sealed in plastic, a pile of towels, two gigantic jars of beauty cream, and huge assorted bottles of vitamins. Still their mother continued to pull out things and put them on the bed—boxes of Ferragamo shoes, leather bags wrapped in pillow cases, designer clothes in their hangers, region 1 DVDs—but their parkas were nowhere. The twins sidled to the door.

The Abominable Snowman

"Where are you going?" their mother demanded.

"Your room." Mikko replied, and he and Martin ran, slamming the door behind them. Their parents' room had a cemented balcony, and although this did mean going out into the open air, they were still technically inside their house and not outside in the street. Besides, they simply wanted to glimpse their unfinished snowman, and to see if the Nemesio children had been successful in making the perfect round head.

As Mikko tugged at the cord that controlled the ceiling-to-floor curtains, Martin ducked behind them and began unlocking the glass doors. Above the swish of the doors, Mikko heard Martin gasp. "It's gone!"

Martin could not believe his eyes. He yelled for his brother to come out and see. Leaving the curtains, Mikko slid out. The twins looked down past their gate and across the street. The spot where they had built their snowman, beside the Nemesio house, lay rather flat and empty.

"No!" Mikko cried out.

Martin clenched his hands and felt the buttons in his left fist. "They messed it up. They destroyed it. They killed it."

Mikko didn't need to ask whom he meant. "We'll make another one and won't let them join."

Nevertheless, their hearts grew heavy. It had taken them more than an hour to make the big and medium-sized balls. They had wanted just to put the finishing touches.

And then Mikko clutched his brother's arm. "But look there, it's alive—"

"It's walking away," Martin added, his voice barely a whisper. They could see something huge and grey, snow-covered, lumbering across the empty lot, away from the spot they had built their snowman. It halted from time to time, and seemed to look down to study itself, and to scuff at the snow, even as more snow fell around him.

"It has feet," Mikko observed, although he couldn't be sure.

"It's trying to cover its tracks," Martin said, shivering.

They looked at each other and ran in, shrieking. Mikko kept tugging at the curtains as Martin slammed the glass doors shut. Their mother walked in. "Mikko, use the cord!" she scolded, then walked over and waved him aside. "Martin, how many times do I have to tell you not to slam—" and then she stopped and looked at her children. "Why were you screaming?" she asked, much more gently.

"Our snowman," Mikko said, gesturing towards the balcony.

"He can walk," Martin said, pointing the same way.

Their mother laughed. "Really? Wow, you've set it free."

The twins shook their heads fearfully.

"You can make it your friend," their mother persisted.

They shook their heads once more.

"Where are our parkas?" Martin asked.

The Abominable Snowman

"We are going to hunt it down." Mikko said.

Once they wore their matching blue and green parkas, they burst out of the house. After an hour on the empty lot, crunching around in the ice-covered talahib, they turned back and decided to build another. The snowfall had ceased by then, successful in obliterating all traces of their snowman. No marks, no footprints, nothing. They could not even say for sure where it had once stood. Martin rang the Nemesios' doorbell, but the eldest Nemesio child, whose name they still did not know, said they were too cold to go out.

So Mikko and Martin built their snowman themselves, finally putting the eyes and the nose just as the sunlight disappeared at around four-thirty in the afternoon. Time and time again, they checked on it from their parents' balcony, to see if it would take a walk, but their second snowman appeared to rest content, just within the perimeter of the Nemesios' garage light.

Mikko and Martin woke up at dawn hearing whispers outside their door. The twins could tell the whispers belonged to their mother and father on the stairs, and waited for them to move away. As soon as the coast was clear, they rushed to their parents' room and out onto the balcony. Their second snowman had stayed, although it looked as if it had sat down. No doubt it had been messed with by one of their adult neighbors, all of whom seemed out on the street with flashlights.

They heard their gate whine open and saw a shape they recognized as their father's go out, just before it clanged shut again. After a minute or so, their mother joined them on the balcony.

"The boy next door, the eldest Inocencio kid, he's missing," their mother said, giving each of them a kiss and a hug. "I'm glad it's not either of you. It would break my heart."

Martin clung to her left arm, and Mikko to her right, as the chill seeped into their cotton pajamas and the ice stung their bare feet.

The Author

CYAN ABAD-JUGO apologizes for setting most of her stories at home or in school, but that is all she has known and thought of so far. She is a very slow thinker and an even slower rememberer. Some of these stories percolated in her head while taking her masters in Children's Literature at Simmons College, Boston, and the rest were written for workshops in UP, which is why she feels indebted to all her teachers, past and present.

The Artist

RANOL is an artist who lives with his eyes set on the stars, his gaze upon the sky, and his hand on the canvas. He is a true son of the mountains whose passion for traveling has taken him to distant lands and peaks that lead to the gates of heaven. And he strums his guitar in a way that only someone who sees the world the way he does can—perfectly.